Baratta's Darkness

By: Marissa Ann & Rae Goldman

Warning:
Credits:
Cover Design by: Francessca's PR & Designs
Editor: Rachel Goldman
Blurb: Melissa Mitchell

ASIN:
ISBN-13: 978-1-7365798-3-1

Poison Pen
Baratta's Darkness
Prologue
Baratta

The club is packed as I make my way to the balcony hoping to get some air. Finding a quiet spot on the far side, I sit and drink my scotch slowly while the boss finishes up his meeting inside. A few minutes goes by when a young woman walks out, stopping to look over the balcony to the street below. New Orleans is always a party town, especially on Saturday night.

She doesn't seem to notice me in the corner, but I happen to be good at blending into the shadows. My eyes are drawn to her, not just by her beauty but by the gorgeous tattoo that goes up one leg disappearing under her short skirt.

"Hey, we all are going to another bar. Want to come with us?" I hear as another woman walks up next to her.

"Nah, I think I'll call it a night soon and go back to the hotel. My flight leaves pretty early." She responds in a sultry husky voice that immediately has me wondering what she would sound like with her legs wrapped around my head.

She stays in the exact same spot for several more minutes after the other girl leaves. As she turns around, she finally notices me as she jumps a little bit and her hand goes to her chest.

"I'm sorry. I didn't see you there." She smiles in my direction.

"I wasn't really trying to be seen." I respond as I take another sip of my scotch.

"Well, sorry." She says as she turns to leave.

"Where are you running off to?" I ask, not really wanting her to leave which is completely out of character for me.

"Back to my hotel. I have an early flight." She smiles again and I catch my breath at her beauty yet again.

What the fuck is wrong with me? I think to myself. I am never impulsive. I calculate everything.

"So you are not from around here then?" I grin back at her as I lean forward, more into the light. I watch as her smile becomes even bigger.

Maybe I won't have to go very far for a fuck tonight after all. Something about this woman has my dick harder than a nail and I don't even know her name.

I convince her to hang out a bit longer. I can't leave until my boss is done with his meeting but I don't tell her that. I offer to buy her a drink instead. I know Uncle Tony won't mind if I slip away after he gets out of here.

Yeah, my boss is also my Uncle. He runs the Italian mob in Louisiana. When my mom died, Uncle Tony and Aunt Morgania took me in. My twin brother went to live with our Grandparents in Italy.

It isn't more than a few minutes later when I see Uncle's bodyguards pushing their way out the front door. He looks up, nodding at me before slipping into his waiting car. The rest of the night is mine. I know exactly where I am going to spend it, or maybe I should say who I am going to spend it in.

Fiona

Today was a huge success for my business. Accepting the invitation to the Inkers Expo they were holding this year in New Orleans was the best decision I could have made. There were so many big names in the business here that would be able to get my name out there. There were several reporters that stopped to take pictures and ask questions about my work.

My dreams were coming true and I had my brother to thank for that. He and his club, The Wolfsbane Ridge MC, gave me my first loan to open up shop after they realized how much I loved to draw and eventually do tattoos. I don't use stencils to do my work, everything is by hand.

Finished with cleanup at my station, I begin packing all of my supplies back into my duffle bags when a couple of the girls I met here walk up asking if I want to go to the after party with them. I think it would be fun, plus hopefully another chance to meet some more people in the business with connections.

"Whew! They are so packed tonight!" Lilyanna comments as we scan for an area to sit.

"Look, there's Clint with some of the others. Let's go up there." Ashley points to the balcony above where there are less people but more of the crowd from the Inkers Expo.

A couple hours later, I decide to get some air as I excuse myself from my friends and head outside. I look out over the street below at all the people walking around and having fun. Some I know are tourists as they stop every so often to take pictures.

I haven't taken a single moment to do the tourist thing. I'm out of time now since I leave tomorrow. Hopefully I can come again just to visit and look around without worrying about work. I think to myself as I watch everyone below.

"Hey, we all are going to another bar. Want to come with us?" asks Ashley as she comes up behind me.

"Nah, I think I'll call it a night soon and go back to the hotel. My flight leaves pretty early."

"Have a safe trip and don't forget about all your new friends now." She says with a smile.

I hug her as we say goodbye. Looking back out over the street below I think about all the new connections this week has brought me. I am truly excited to get back home and get started on all the new bookings I have for next week.

As I turn around a guy in the corner catches my eye and I jump a little not expecting to see anyone. Has he been there the whole time? I ask myself.

I smile to be polite at the handsome stranger but when he steps out into the light. Oh My God! My panties drop and I let loose a real smile. This man could probably rock my world. I want!

I've never had a one night stand before but I think that is about to change, there is no way I am letting this guy get away without revealing that impressive bulge I can see straining against his pants.

"Hi, I am Fiona, but my friends all call me Fee." I tell him as I extend my hand for a shake.

"Baratta" he says and when he reaches out to shake my hand I check for a wedding ring. No ring, my clit is doing a happy dance. Good thing we are standing, my panties are so wet now, sitting would be uncomfortable.

Chapter 1
Fiona

I grew up in White Summer Montana but I had big dreams, I was going to see the world. First chance I got I was out of here. Turns out the world isn't that wonderful without your family at your side. So after a messy relationship ended I decided it was time to come home.

I made a name for myself. People from all around the globe came to me for tattoos. They would come to me in White Summer just like they did in Seattle.

I knew my brother's club had been having some issues but I was an outsider and always would be, it didn't bother me. He had his life and I had mine. Just being close gave me the security and comfort I need.

I know that if I ever need them the Timberwolves MC would be here for me. They even loaned me the start-up to help transfer my shop here.

On my first trip home to get the ball rolling, the club was in chaos. They had visitors from out of town. That's when I saw HIM.

It's been two years since New Orleans but I'll never forget the man that rocked my world then disappeared into thin air. After going back to my hotel we spent the night wrapped up in each other. Finally falling asleep in the early hours of dawn. I only slept a couple hours and when I woke up he was gone.

It was a good thing I had packed before going out with the girls. I barely had time to grab my stuff and get to the airport before my flight back to Seattle. I slept the entire way. I daydreamed about him often but never thought I would actually see him again. Especially not here.

He didn't even try to talk to me. I actually think he went out of his way to avoid me. Then he was gone again, like a ghost. Appearing and disappearing from my life.

Baratta

When Uncle Tony informed me that we were headed back to White Summer Montana to attend the grand opening of the Poison Pen, I felt as if I were punched in the gut.

Very similar to the way I felt when our eyes connected that day several months ago when she came strolling into the Wolfsbane Ridge club house.

Finding out that her brother was the sergeant at arms for the club whose girls had been kidnapped and sold into trafficking by Joey, surprised the hell out of me. And I don't like fucking surprises!

I tried to make excuses as to why I should stay in New Orleans but none of them worked. Uncle Tony was going to relent but Aunt Morgania got that little shit eating grin on her face right before she told Uncle that she would only feel completely safe if I were there with them.

So here I am at the airport loading our bags into the rental car as Uncle calls to check on our reservations at Wolf's Ridge which is owned by the club.

"Our cabins are ready for us. After we drop off our luggage you can leave me at the clubhouse. I have a meeting scheduled with Timber. I think your Aunt wants you to take her into town." Uncle Tony looks over at my Aunt with raised brows.

"Yes please. If it's not too much trouble for you Baratta. All the girls are at Bella's Brew."

"It's not a problem Aunty." I say while looking at her through the rearview mirror which makes her smile.

Calling her Aunty in private has always put a smile on her face. No one outside our family knows the truth of who I am. I prefer it that way so that those I love can not be used against me.

The kind of work that I am in comes with hazards that can get my family killed. Hell, it can get me killed. I don't worry about any of that though. I have zero guilt when it comes to putting a bullet into someone. I actually never think of them again.

While I don't feel shit when it comes to others, I know my rage would take over if anything happened to my Aunt and Uncle. My cousin too.

I'm really fond of Markayla. She was always really sweet to me when we were younger. The other kids and even the teachers treated me like shit. They said something was wrong with me.

Especially after the day I hit another kid in the head with a rock busting his head open. He had pushed Markayla down on the playground making her knee bleed. I refused to say I was sorry for what I did to him because hell, I wasn't sorry at all.

All these years later and I'm still not sorry.

Fiona

I didn't sleep at all last night, today is opening day at Poison Pen. It's still early so I am sitting at the counter at Bella's coffee shop. I thought it would calm me down but it's just adding to my already frazzled nerves.

Bella and Mina are sitting on either side of me, for moral support. Bella is sucking down coffee like it's going out of style. I suppose having two babies at home, she needs the caffeine. Victory is a newborn and Justice is teething.

I am just about to ask where Miranda and Hayden are, when they come walking in the door. "Speak of the devil." I say instead.

"Huh?" They both look at me.

"I was just about to ask about the two of you." I reply as they join us.

Hayden orders a coffee from Bella's mom but Miranda just asks for water. We all turn to look at her; she immediately gives us a shy grin.

"Well you know how me and Blood decided to try for a baby? My doctor said caffeine is bad for him or her." She says with a sly grin. It takes a minute for her meaning to sink into my already frazzled nerves but then I understand.

"OH MY GOD!" I scream, "I am going to be an Aunt!"

We all jump up surrounding Miranda, all of us giving her congratulations and hugs. When it's my turn I wrap my arms around my new sister and burst into tears. Now everybody is hugging me instead.

The words, "don't cry" make it through my sobbing but I explain they are happy tears.

"I am just so happy. Today I open my new shop and find out I have a new niece or nephew on the way. There is nothing that can ruin my day now."

Maybe I spoke too soon.

Baratta

I drop off my Uncle at the Wolfsbane clubhouse so he can meet with Timber and the guys. They still have some things to work out. Uncle Tony asked me to drive Aunt Morgania to Bella's Brew where the girls are supposed to be hanging out today.

Through the window I watch as Morgania joins the women. Delilah, Bella's mom, is serving customers and refilling coffee cups. I'm about to go sit in the car where I can watch them without being in the way when Fiona turns to look out the window.

I immediately notice her red eyes and tear streaked face. Something about her kicks my protective instincts into overdrive and I storm into the shop ready to kill whatever has caused such distress to her. Before I even think about what I am doing I grab her chin so she can't look away.

"What's wrong? Why are you crying? Did someone hurt you?" The questions just fly out of my mouth and then she starts laughing.

My hands drop and I step back. A minute ago she was balling her eyes out and now she is laughing? She is laughing ... at me. Dear Lord, she is insane. Going from one extreme to the other, what the hell have I walked into? I look around at Bella, Mina, Miranda and that Hayden chick that runs the local gym and they are all laughing.

My Aunt pushes me to the side and hugs Fiona. "What's wrong, dear?"

"Nothing is wrong. These are happy tears. I am going to be an Aunt." she says as she wipes her eyes one more time.

Aunt Morgania looks at each of the women one at a time, and they all shake their heads. Until she gets to Miranda, who nods.

I feel a weight lift off my chest. When did I care so much about this woman's tears? I barely know her yet I was ready to kill whoever made her cry. I start to back out of the store but Morgania stops me to ask if I'll go with Fiona over to her shop so she can prepare for opening.

I try to convince Aunt Morgania that I need to stay and protect her but she looks at the women and says, "Who is packing." every hand in the group goes up. I know when I am outnumbered. So I concede by asking Fiona if she is ready to go.

Fiona

Why the fuck is he here? I think to myself as he holds the passenger side door open for me. I knew the club had extended the invitation to Mr. Marcus and we girls have stayed in touch with Morgania so naturally we expected them. But did they honestly have to bring him along?

I know that I am being a little petty. He seems to be their body guard or something. I've never really asked what exactly he does. I do know one thing for sure. The Marcus family is a well known Mob organization.

"Pull around to the back please." I point to the driveway leading to the back parking lot as we come up to the shop.

When he stops, I don't wait for him to get out and open my door. I quickly jump out and head for the building. The less time I am in his company the better.

Reaching the landing of the stairs that lead up to the attached apartment that I moved into, I hear him get out and walk across the gravel behind me.

"You don't have to come up. Thank you for the ride though." I look back at him and think that maybe I shouldn't have. My eyes are glued to his just as they were that very first night and I feel as though I can't get enough air into my lungs.

"I am sure Blood would appreciate me checking everything out before I just leave you all alone." The corner of his mouth lifts as he walks around me going up the stairs to my door.

Instead of saying anything else to the stubborn ass, I follow him up the stairs. Reaching the door I notice there is a package with my name on it. Picking it up, I take it inside with me.

"Did you really not lock the door while you were gone?" Baratta asks as he walks into the kitchen.

"This is White Summer, not Seattle or New Orleans. If anything happens here, my brother takes care of it." I shrug my shoulders as I reach to open the box that was left for me on the porch.

As it opens up, I remove the tissue paper that is on top to reveal what looks to be a cut out of me from a picture that was taken. But the picture is clearly from when I was in the shower as you can see the water running down my back. In bold black ink down my back someone has written MINE.

"What the fuck?" I breathe out as all I can do is look at it. Baratta's hand comes from beside me grabbing the cutout and examining it.

"I am going to assume that you did not willingly pose for this picture?" Baratta says through gritted teeth. I am unsure if he is pissed about the picture or the thought that I would actually willingly pose for it.

"Of course not!" As I reach out to grab the picture from him hoping to hide it, I see more writing on the back. In angry red letters it says, "Did you think you could leave me behind?"

I sink down into a chair as a cold chill seems to start at my toes and move up my body. Baratta is so busy looking at the picture and ignoring me that he doesn't even notice when I put my head between my knees and struggle to breathe.

"So, it's a threat then." He states matter of factly.

"We don't know if it's a threat. There isn't a note in the box." I snap back. I don't know if it's his attitude, his presence or what it is but just seconds ago I was on the verge of a panic attack. Now I just want to hit him and make him leave.

"You are not naive Fi, so don't act like it. We need to let your brother and his club know about this."

"Absolutely not! There is no need to get them involved just yet. We don't even know what this is anyway."

I know I should do what he says and tell my family. However; I'm still hurt by the way he left me in New Orleans and especially pissed about him just disappearing the last time he was here without so much as a word.

"Okay. If you don't want to tell them then the only thing left to do is for me to stay here with you. I will let Uncle know and we can go pick up my suitcase from the cabin." He talks so calmly as if it is all settled.

"No. You are not staying here with me. And did you just say Uncle? I didn't know you brought your Uncle with you."

Baratta

Oh fuck, I have never slipped and called Tony, Uncle in front of anyone before. It's not like I can pretend I didn't say it. She clearly heard me. I run my hands over my face and through my hair in frustration. What is it about this woman that lowers all my carefully built walls?

"Listen to me and listen closely," I growl as I grab her shoulders. "Tony and Morgania are my Uncle and Aunt. You can't tell anyone! Not your brother! Not his club! Not your girl club! Nobody can know this! Not ever!"

For the first time ever Fiona looks frightened of me, but I can't let this closely guarded secret get out. Now I have to stay not just for her protection but the safety of my family as well.

I will kill to keep my family safe and for some reason my heart is including her. I'm not willing to examine that just yet. At least not out loud. She'd fight me on it. On that thought maybe I would like to voice it out loud in front of her.

I step back and look into her eyes. The fire that was missing a few minutes ago is back. She thinks I didn't notice her on the edge, I see everything. It is the way I was trained. I knew if I gave in and showed compassion she would be a sobbing mess.

I prefer when my woman fights with me and next to me. I don't want her to be a delicate little flower. She doesn't know it yet but this little gift just sealed the deal. She is mine and I am not leaving her again.

Chapter 2
Fiona

I glance at the wall clock and notice the time. "Shit I've gotta go! I need to let the caterers and my employees in downstairs."

Grabbing my bags and keys, I am ready to dash for the door until Baratta grabs my hand to stop me.

"Don't forget what I said."

"Yeah, Yeah I gotta go."

"I am not leaving you alone until someone else gets here." He tells me.

"I don't care if you glue yourself to my ass; I have a business to run. DO NOT get in my way!"

He releases my hand and steps back. "Lead the way."

I'm half way down the steps when he asks me if I have a key for the apartment, I don't answer just dangle the keys over my shoulder. He must understand my meaning because he finally catches up to say he locked the door.

I'm unlocking the shop door when I hear a vehicle pull into the back lot; I know it has to be the caterer. For my grand opening tonight I have finger foods and alcohol available. I was going to just do drinks but Mina insisted on there being food, and nobody says no to Mina.

After showing them where to set up, I go get my work space ready. I'm in the zone almost forgetting that Baratta is even here. Dancing to the music while setting up my work station, I jump out of my skin when there is a tap on my shoulder. Shit, I drop the bottle of ink in my hand and spin around.

"Just thought you would want to know your girls are pounding on the front door. You really should be more aware of your surroundings Fi."

"You really should wear a freaking bell." I mutter sarcastically under my breath as I walk to the door and let the girls in.

Morgania is the only one that hasn't been here before, so I leave her to wander exploring the shop while I grab for the book in Mina's hand. Mina pulls away, "Uh uh, you don't get to see it yet."

"But Mina, it's my appointment book. I need to know what I'm in for tonight." I whine playfully. She's been taking my calls and setting my appointments while I prepared the shop.

I was going to do it myself but she begged saying she was bored since she has time off for a little while. Her most recent book was released a few weeks ago and she hasn't started a new one yet.

Baratta

The caterers are loading tables with food trays, and Mina is playing keep away with Fiona's appointment book when I hear the back door open. I do a quick look and see that everyone that is supposed to be here is already here, so I go on alert.

There is a doorway in the back that leads to a short hallway before reaching the backdoor. I quickly make my way there to block whoever is trying to sneak in the back. The two people are so busy talking to each other they don't even notice me until one of the women bounces off my chest.

"Ummm Fi!" she calls out. "Did you hire a bouncer?"

I just stand there staring down at her. The other woman she is with clears her throat. "Uh Um Fi" she shouts. Then I feel Fiona's small hands on my hips trying to move me out of the way.

I can't help but laugh, she thinks she can make me move. It's short lived though because her hands on my body are making me think of other things we could be doing.

"Damnit Baratta, get out of the way and let my employees in." Fi says

Reluctantly, I move to the side. If Fi keeps touching me I might throw her over my shoulder and carry her back upstairs, her grand opening be damned.

"Introduce me to your employees" I say when I step to the side.

"This itty bitty woman in front of you is Lilyanna; you might remember her from New Orleans. She is the second best tattoo artist in the world." She says dramatically like this is all a game.

"And the lady behind her is our apprentice Arin. Now move, we still have work to do before we open in less than an hour."

Fiona

That man is so infuriating, I want to stomp my feet while screaming but I am not a child so instead I choose to ignore him. Grabbing Lily and Arin by the hand, I drag them to the front of the shop where my other friends are waiting.

"Ladies, please meet my employees. This is Lilyanna, I call her Lily and she is the second best tattoo artist in the world." Then I nudge Arin forward. "This is Arin, our apprentice."

Bella is the only one that takes my bait, "Who is the first best tattoo artist in the world?"

"Me. of course." I answer as we all break out in laughter.

"Stepped right in that one didn't I?" Bella says.

"O.K Ladies we have thirty minutes to finish our prep before I unlock the doors." Lily goes to her station and Arin follows to watch as she sets out her inks, making sure all her equipment is in working order.

"Mina, no more playing I need my appointment book and notes so I know what I am doing tonight."

"Nope." she says. "Tonight you are tattooing Timber, Blade and Blood." Then she slips a piece of paper out of her pocket. I look at it in shock. It is the Wolfsbane Ridge logo.

"For the next two weeks, you are doing the club members. I have a few randos scheduled for Lily and Arin but the club trusts nobody but you."

I'm so overwhelmed with happiness and gratitude. I feel like my heart will burst. This has been such a drastic move for me and I've been hiding my anxiety. But; I know I won't fail. I have my family around me again and nothing is going to get in the way of my success.

I step into the bathroom to fix my makeup and take a few deep breaths. This day has gone by in the blink of an eye but now this last fifteen minutes seems to have slowed to a snail's pace. I can hear all the activity happening in the shop through the thin walls.

I just stand there for a few minutes pulling myself together. Suddenly all the sounds in the shop go quiet and there is a knock at the door. "Fi" Mina's voice calls out. "Fi, it's time." I take one more deep breath, as I steady my shaking hands and then open the door.

As I walk out into the shop, every eye in the room is on me. This is my moment, my dream and my reality.

"OK bitches open those doors!" I call out. Hayden is standing just inside the door. She gives me a wink then turns flipping the lock.

As the door opens, I can see there are only about ten people standing out there. I'm confused as to why there aren't more but then I hear it. The roar of motorcycles coming into town.

We all step outside to watch as they pull in and I can see a line of cars behind them. In just a matter of minutes my parking lot is overflowing and both sides of the street are lined with vehicles.

Timber steps off his bike, quickly joined by Blood and Blade on either side of him. It's almost as if Timber is the pied piper, leading the group to my door. I notice that Blood isn't looking at me but over my shoulder and he doesn't look very happy.

A quick glance tells me why. Baratta is standing right behind me with his arms crossed looking like an intimidating statue. I spin around with a glare.

"I told you I am not leaving your side."

"You are going to scare my customers away!" I hiss.

When I turn around my brother, Blood is right there. He lifts me off my feet in a big hug, spinning me around. I'm giggling like a schoolgirl when he sets me back down.

"Welcome to Poison Pen." I call out to everyone before stepping back through the door, followed by what seems to be a hundred people.

The first hour is spent meeting and greeting everyone. I was a little worried about how they would react to a tattoo shop because of the bad rep some shops have brought into a community. But, I'm warmly welcomed. Most of these people know me, we grew up together and they are happy for my success.

I'm talking to Tony and Morgania when there's a tap at my shoulder.

"It's time." Lily says. So I excuse myself as I go look for Timber because he is up first.

Baratta

I have been sticking to the shadows, like the ghost some people call me, watching Fi mingle in the crowd. I haven't seen anything suspicious yet but this is a big group so I'm not sure if I've seen everyone. I need more eyes, only Fiona won't tell her brother about the so-called gift. Therefore I have to be vigilant.

I'm about to approach her, when Lily says something in her ear. She looks around zeroing in on Timber. Excusing herself from the conversation she was having with my Aunt and Uncle, she motions to him to follow her to her work station.

With her occupied in one area, I can concentrate a little easier on the guests that's milling around. There seems to be so many that it is virtually impossible.

"Why are you watching my baby sister so closely?" Blood growls from behind me. I knew he was there before he even spoke. He's been watching me since he got here with the others.

"No particular reason. I'm watching all the guests. After all, I'm here to protect Mr. and Mrs. Marcus. You never know where there will be a potential threat."

"Yet, I know that you were already here before they even got here. So tell me, why exactly you are staying so close to Fi." I can hear anger bubbling up although he keeps a tight grip on himself. I admire that.

"I need to check out the layout ahead of time. Fiona was generous enough to allow me to do that in the hours before the opening." Shrugging my shoulders as if it were not a big deal.

"You just keep your eyes and your hands to yourself where she is concerned."

"I get this overwhelming feeling that you do not like me, Blood. What exactly have I done to offend you?" I ask as I turn my full attention on him.

"Just stay away from her." He demands through gritted teeth before walking away.

"You sure know how to piss that one off." My Uncle says from my other side.

"He's protective of his sister. An admirable trait. I can respect that."

"Does that mean you will stay away from the girl?"

"No." Is the only answer I give before I head toward Fiona's workstation. I can hear Uncle Tony laugh as I stride away. I'm sure he is dying to ask me more but he won't. He knows me well enough to know that when I am ready to let him know anything, I will do so without any prodding.

Fiona

Half way done with Timber's tat, I feel uneasy as if I am being watched. I know that it is a stupid feeling. Because of course I'm being watched. There are guests everywhere coming and going, sometimes looking over my shoulder as I work. It's never bothered me before though.

I know the second Baratta's eyes land on me. My skin prickles and I feel my nipples tighten up. The way that man makes my body react is just insane. I have never met another who has ever made me feel like he does. It pisses me the fuck off too.

Although it would not piss me off if we finally got a round two. I think to myself as I raise my eyes looking directly into his. The corner of his mouth lifts as if he can read my thoughts. I just smile back before lowering my head back to my work.

"You might want to stop smiling at him like that. Your brother looks ready to slit his damn throat as it is." Timber whispers on a chuckle.

"My brother should mind his own damn business."

"So it's like that is it?"

I look up at Timber and I know his meaning so I give him a slight nod. I like Baratta even though I would never admit it to him. He's infuriating as hell and a pain in my ass. But my brother has no say in who I sleep with or have a relationship with.

I've no idea if Baratta or even myself is interested in a relationship, but I'm for damn sure interested in getting that man back into my bed for a few hours. It's been too long since I've felt as good as he made me feel in New Orleans. I'm still pissed though that he left me before I even woke up. I very nearly missed my plane that morning.

"I'll try to keep your brother in check but you will need to talk to him eventually Fi. He's your brother and you two are all each other have, besides the club."

"I know and I will. He also needs to remember that I am grown. I moved away last time because I needed a life of my own without interference from him. Hell, I went to prom alone because all the guys in my class were afraid of the club. I won't let any of you keep me from having a social life now that I am older."

"I'll promise to try to keep all the brothers in line if you stop digging that needle in so hard." He grits out.

"Sorry." I scrunch my face up and he just shakes his head at me.

I finish the rest of the shading before I scoot back to look over my work. It still amazes me to see my own art on another person. I don't think I will ever get completely used to it.

"That looks awesome half-pint!" Blade says as he walks over to the table.

"I think she gets even better each time she works." Timber comments looking over it himself.

"Can't wait to get mine too." Wrench walks in with a smile. He's been a little quieter since coming back home from the armed forces. I'm just glad he came home just like the rest of the club.

Around two in the morning I am at the door, saying goodnight to all of my guests as they begin to leave. It was a really great night but now I am tired and ready to call it a night.

"Don't forget the family BBQ. Some of the other clubs that are here will have their families with them. So you'll get a chance to see some of the people that didn't come tonight." My brother says, standing in the doorway. Apparently he's the last one out although his eyes keep scanning the area behind me.

"Are you looking for something?" I cross my arms over my chest as I glare at him.

"No. Everything looks as it should. Just don't forget to lock up. I know how forgetful you are about that." I roll my eyes even though I know he is right.

"Yes sir, I will as soon as you walk out." I sweetly droll out.

He shakes his head at me, closes the door behind him but I see him stop to watch me until I turn the lock. A few minutes later he drives off on his bike following Timber back to the clubhouse.

"Did you have a good night?" I hear whispered next to my ear causing me to jump with a gasp.

"Fuck. I thought you left. You scared the hell out of me!" I shove at his shoulder although it doesn't move him at all.

Baratta

"I told you I wasn't leaving Fi." I murmur looking into her eyes.

The look she gave me earlier had my balls tightening up in my pants. I swear the woman is a witch. No other has ever captured my attention like she has.

"Well if you are staying, I guess we will eat some leftovers and watch a movie." She walks away leaving me to follow her. Which I do of course. I will follow her to the ends of the Earth; she just doesn't know it yet.

I watch as she locks the back door before we head up the stairs to her apartment. I really do try to not watch her ass as she walks in front of me but I can't seem to help myself where she is concerned.

When she stops to unlock the door, I crowd close to her back and its pure torture feeling her ass so close to my cock even with clothes on. I know that I affect her just as much as she affects me if her breathing is any indication.

Light spills out of her apartment door when she finally gets it opened and that is when we notice the box sitting to the right of the door outside. Her back stiffens when she notices it.

"Just go inside Fi. I'll look it over first." I murmur as I lean down to look at it carefully before touching it.

Surprisingly, she doesn't argue which is so unlike her but she's probably tired. I can hear her in the kitchen as she starts opening up the fridge. Taking my knife from my boot, I flip it open, slicing the tape that is holding the box closed.

Inside there is a picture. Only this one is not just of Fiona. In this picture I'm standing next to her looking off into the crowd as she looks up at me with a thoughtful expression. They took a black sharpie trying to scratch out my image and wrote MINE in bold letters all around her.

"So another one then?" Fiona asks as I walk in shutting the door. She walks over, taking the box from me and looking inside.

"Who the hell could be doing this?" She whispers as if to herself. Shaking her head, she drops it back into the box before grabbing a bowl of popcorn.

"Thought you were going to eat some real food instead of junk? And where are you going?" I ask, watching her walk down the hall.

"My bedroom is the only room with a TV if you haven't noticed. So if you are going to watch a movie with me, it'll have to be in there. And popcorn is real food." She smiles before disappearing into the bedroom on the left.

Watch a movie with her in her bedroom? Where there happens to be a bed? *Oh fuck me.* I think to myself then *Yes Please.*

Chapter 3
Fiona

I wake up feeling arms wrapped around me and immediately know who it is. I was expecting to wake up alone again just like the last time we were together, although nothing happened between us last night. I'm pretty sure I fell fast asleep the first thirty minutes into the movie.

Moving slightly, I can feel his hard body at my back. I certainly do not miss the even harder erection that is straining through his clothes at my ass. Unable to resist, I press my ass back into him as I slowly move my hips to rub his length.

"Fi." I hear him growl as his hand grabs my side. At first I think he is going to stop me but instead, he pushes even harder into my ass and I can't help but moan.

His hand slides up my side to cup my breast. He gently squeezes then his fingers move to my nipple pinching the already hard nub. I turn over facing him and push his hand away. I have to know the truth before this goes any further.

Sitting up, I adjust myself making sure no skin is exposed. He gives me a confused look but seems to know I am about to say something. Taking a few breaths, I just let it out.

"Why did you leave me?"

"What do you mean, why did I leave? I didn't leave."

"Yes you did, I woke up in New Orleans and you were gone. I almost missed my flight to Seattle and you were gone."

He reaches up to wipe away a tear that I didn't even know was there. "Fi, Fiona I didn't leave you. I went to get coffee. When I got back you were gone."

He continues, "I tried to find you. I only had your first name and knew that you were an artist. I didn't even know where you called home. Imagine my surprise when you walked into the Wolfsbane Ridge clubhouse after two years."

He didn't leave me! He didn't leave me. He is going on and on about trying to find me and my shocked brain just keeps repeating, he didn't leave me. Pure joy rocks through my system as I throw my arms around his neck and kiss him to shut him up.

I can't get close enough to him; I want to feel his skin against mine. I want all of him and I want him now. Thank God he slept in only his boxers, so there isn't much to remove because I need to get him naked.

He pulls his lips from mine but I follow and don't let him get away. Baratta laughs, that is what stops me. He is laughing at me? I finally pull back into an almost pout.

"Fiona, neither of us is going to get our clothes off if our lips are locked together and I need to grab a condom."

I don't bother getting out of bed. Pulling my tank top off, I throw it across the room before yanking my sleep shorts down my legs until I am completely naked.

"Well I guess you took care of that problem." he laughs as he gets up. Reaching into his jeans, he grabs a foil pack out of his pocket before stepping out of his boxer shorts then getting back in the bed with me.

With our lips meeting again I try to show him just how much I've missed him. Longed for him even over the last two years. His hands find my breasts to pinch at my nipples making them ache for even more. My body is going up in flames, a fire I've long since learned that only he can put out.

He starts kissing down my neck and across my collar bone moving slowly down with each touch, until he gets to the hard tips of my breasts. He sucks my nipple into his mouth devouring it as his hands move even lower on my body.

His fingers find my clit, sending shockwaves through me but he doesn't stop there. His lips are still moving down my body kissing his way right down to my pussy. Looking down at him as his head finds its way between my legs; I feel his tongue flick at my clit before sucking on it hard.

I grab his hair in both hands, pushing up with my hips to feel more of his tongue and pulling with my hands trying to get him closer. As I begin to think I can't take any more he puts two fingers inside of me. The combination of his tongue on my clit and his fingers in my pussy sends me over the edge. My orgasm explodes out of me as I scream his name.

Sinking back into the bed to catch my breath, our eyes meet. He has a feral grin on his face. In all my experiences I have never had a man look at me like that after eating my pussy. He slides back up so we are face to face.

"We are not done yet."

"You are right. It is my turn." I say and lower my hands as I scoot down until my face is even with his cock. Licking the shaft, while not taking my eyes off his, I then open my mouth slowly sucking in the tip. I'm about to plunge down when he grabs me by my hair, pulling me back up.

"Uh Uh, not this time. It's been too long since I felt your pussy wrapped around me and I want to be inside you when I come." he tells me. I pout as he laughs at me again. "Next time Fi, you can do whatever you want to me next time. But, I need to be inside you now."

He slides me to the side reaching for the condom, but I snatch it out of his hand. Ripping open the foil I take the condom out and reach for him, "Allow me." Using both hands I slip it over the head of his cock sliding it down into place. Teasing and caressing him as I go.

He grabs me under both arms lifting me up beside him again.

"Woman, you are going to drive me crazy!" Rolling until he is on top, he takes both my wrists holding them over my head.

"This is mine." He shouts as he plunges his cock deep inside me.

I yell out at the sudden intrusion but more from surprise than anything else. He slowly pulls back out and shakes his head.

"I'm sorry baby but this is going to be fast. I've missed you too much to take my time." He thrust back in, I can already feel him throbbing and dancing inside me, so I know he is really close to his own release.

My pussy seems to have the same intentions as I'm on the edge ready to milk him dry. Meeting each one of his thrusts with one of my own, I feel him hitting that secret spot inside my wet pussy. The sudden sharp pain of him hitting against my cervix makes me gasp but it is not enough to make me stop; it only adds to my already building climax.

He leans down, biting my nipple causing me to completely lose it. Moaning and thrashing below him. My pussy feels like it is milking him for everything he has got. I whimper as he slowly pulls out.

"Did I hurt you?"

"No, you filled me up. Taking all the space inside me but now, I feel empty without you."

We both lay in bed just holding each other until a sudden noise makes me jump.

"Oh shit." I clutch my chest then break out laughing when I realize it is the alarm on my phone.

Baratta

We were cocooned in our own little heaven until the alarm on her phone went off. I know I have shit to do today but I don't want to go out into the real world just yet. When she reaches for her phone I pull her back into my arms kissing her. She reaches up wrapping herself around my neck.

Just when I think we might go for a second round my own phone pings. I want to ignore it but I can't. Uncle Tony might need me. So with another peck on her lips I pull away. Rolling out of bed I swipe up my phone telling Fi, "Sorry I have to take it."

While I am talking to Uncle Tony, she gets up heading for the bathroom so I wander out to her kitchen deciding to start a pot of coffee. By the time she is done in the shower I have two cups on the table ready to go.

"I am not sure how you take your coffee, but I couldn't find any cream or sugar."

"Black is perfect." hmmm her little moan when she takes that first sip makes my cock hard but we both have things to do.

"What is your schedule today?" I ask, but she just gives me a blank look.

"What? Why?"

"Because I am not leaving you alone. I told you as long as you keep getting those creepy ass pictures I am not leaving. So tell me your schedule."

She takes a deep breath, I know she is going to argue with me on this, but then she lets out a sigh. "I want to fight you, I really do. However; I know you are going to do whatever the hell you want anyways. I have kickboxing at Hayden's then lunch with my friends before I open the shop at two."

While I get dressed, Fiona grabs the things she needs, before we walk out the door together. "Keys" I call out to her as she retreats down the stairs. She dangles them over her shoulder like she did yesterday, so I make sure her door is locked.

I leave her at the door to the Den, Hayden's gym, before heading out to the Wolfsbane Ridge clubhouse. Uncle Tony and Aunt Morgania are saying their goodbyes when I arrive.

After driving them twenty minutes to a private airport where their bodyguards are already waiting, I pull Uncle Tony aside.

"I'm staying here."

He starts laughing, not just a snicker but a full on belly laugh.

"Boy." He claps me on the shoulder, "you just lost me ten thousand dollars."

"And you are happy about this?" Confusion written on my face.

"Your Aunt told me you would stay behind. I did not believe her."

"Something is going on Uncle Tony. Yesterday she received two packages at her apartment. They were creepy pictures, one was her in the shower, and the other was from her opening. They both had the word mine written over her body." Uncle Tony is no longer laughing.

"Does her brother know?"

"No, she doesn't want to tell anyone. If I hadn't been there I wouldn't know."

"You have my blessing to stay. I will call in your brother to take your place, for now."

"Thank you, Uncle."

I leave him at the steps to his plane but as I am walking back to the car he shouts, "You better have a good excuse for Blood; he is protective of his little sister."

I head back to town but decide to stop at the clubhouse first. Blood happens to be the one to meet me at the door.

"What are you doing back?" He wants to know, but I don't owe him any answers.

"Is Timber available?" I demand from him, "Take me to your leader."

I can see that he really doesn't want me there. However; since I asked for Timber he has no choice but to escort me to the President's office. After knocking on the door, he lets Timber know I want to speak to him before he rounds on me himself.

"Leave Fiona alone!" he says through gritted teeth.

"Not going to happen." I reply before walking around him to greet Timber. I get a small bit of childish satisfaction from shutting the door in his face.

"You have cameras in this town?" I ask before Timber even has a chance to greet me.

"Yes, why?"

"I want eyes on Fiona's apartment and Poison Pen at all times."

"Is there a problem?" he sits up straighter; I have his complete attention now. Since Fiona doesn't want the club to know, I have to be creative about my reasons. I just wish that woman was not so stubborn.

"She is a single woman that gets off work between midnight and two a.m. Do I need more reason than that?"

Timber runs his hands through his hair. "You are right. You would tell me if there was a problem wouldn't you?"

"If I could, I would." I hedge a little. He sees right through me, but also knows I won't give him more than that. Noticing the time on the clock behind him, I make my exit but just before going through the door I call back, "Oh yeah, I will be staying in town for a while." I can hear him cursing all the way from the parking lot.

I get back into town with enough time to swing by the hardware store. I plan to upgrade Fiona's locks and security on both the apartment plus the shop. Then I go by Hay's Den to pick her up.

There must be a class this morning, as I see a few motorcycles parked on the street and Mina's car in the lot. Making my way inside, I hear yelling and cheering. Curiosity makes me walk back to the main part of the gym, where the boxing ring is.

Nothing could surprise me more than what my eyes see in the ring. Fiona is wearing nothing but short shorts and a sports bra with her hands wrapped. The surprising part is the big guy in the ring getting his ass kicked by my girl. I've met Austin before and he is nothing to joke about. He's a former MMA fighter, almost as big as me.

Mina, Bella, Hayden and Miranda are yelling and cheering her on. I reach for Bella's shoulder to ask her what is going on, but before I make contact Blade is standing between us. "Do not touch my old lady!" I raise my hands and step back. "I was only going to ask her about this." as I gesture towards the ring. "I would never hurt a woman." I assure him.

"What is going on is Fiona is kicking Austin's ass."

"But why?"

"Because she can." Mina interrupts, "Now shut up so we can cheer for our girl."

Stepping back I nod my head to the side signaling for Blade to follow me. As soon as we step out I ask him, "Are you going to be with the ladies through lunch?"

"Yes, on self defense days they all go to Bella's after class, why?"

"Can you do me a solid and keep an eye on Fiona, until I get back? I have a few things to do."

"Yeah I got you man. Even if you don't see them, there is always someone watching our females."

I nod my thanks before heading back to Fiona's building.

When I get there, I find a manila envelope taped to her door. I'm not worried about breaking in, since I'm going to replace the locks anyways. So I jimmy the door open.

I pour the envelope out on her table. There must be a hundred pictures here and they are not all from the last two days.

On top of the stack is a picture of her at the Inkers expo, then one of her on the balcony where we met. As I go through them it is like the story of her life for the last two years. Every single picture has the word MINE written in black and red sharpie on it.

Scooping the pics back into the envelope adding the two previous ones she received, I look around trying to find the perfect place to hide them before I get to work fixing the locks.

I'm just finishing up when I hear someone at the door. Reaching for my gun, I yank the door open.

I must have lost track of time because Fiona stumbles in with her brother right behind her.

"What the Hell! Why didn't my key work?" Tossing her the new keys I explain everything I've done.

"All the doors and windows have new locks. Upstairs and downstairs. There is a security light above your door that is motion activated. If you give me your phone, I'll download the app to your doorbell so you can see everybody that rings it." I don't tell her about the cameras I installed here or in the shop. I also don't tell her about the newest delivery I've hidden away because her brother will flip his lid.

"I have to get ready for work." Is the only thing she says when she drops her gym bag on the couch while heading to the bedroom to change. As soon as she is out of the room, Blood confronts me.

"Why are you here? Why did you do this for my sister? Where are you staying? When are you leaving?"

"Slow down man, I can only answer one question at a time. Number one, none of your business, number two because she is a woman alone that works late at night, number three and four... none of your fucking business."

Fiona

I can hear Blood and Baratta's raised voices through my bedroom door while I'm changing. I know my brother is overprotective of me, but if Baratta is staying they need to get along. I love my brother but my sex life is mine.

As soon as I step out of my bedroom, Blood is right there. "Why is he here?"

"Because I asked him to be." is the only answer I give him. It's not the full truth but it is all the truth my brother is going to get.

I take a deep steadying breath because I know Blood is only trying to watch out for me. He always has, always will.

"Blood, I'm twenty four years old. I moved to Seattle for my apprenticeship when I was only nineteen. I've lived on my own and made my own decisions for five years now. You have to trust me to live my life. Baratta is staying. Period."

"You just met him! How can you expect me to trust him with my sister?"

"Blood, Blood" I have to say his name a couple of times before he focuses back on me. "That is not true; I met him two years ago." My brother looks at me as if I just told him the moon was made of blue cheese.

"Is he the reason you came home?"

"No. I came home because I want to be home. I miss my family. I miss you and if I was not here, I would miss my soon-to-be niece or nephew."

"If he hurts you I'll kill him. I don't care who he works for!"

"Blood, if he hurts me I'll kill him. You have seen me in the ring; you also taught me how to shoot.

I can take care of myself. Please Blood, back off, for me."

Blood looks over to Baratta, "You heard my sister. Hurt her and you are a dead man." Then he storms out the door.

Baratta doesn't say a word; he just pulls me into his arms and holds me. After a few moments I swear I hear him say, "Thank you." but I don't know what he is thanking me for, so I say nothing.

My phone pings telling me I have a text so I untangle myself from his arms to check my phone. It's from my brother.

"Be at the shooting range at 9 a.m. Saturday. Prove to me you still got it."

It's time to open the shop, so I grab my keys and we head down stairs. "Baratta, I need a shop key for Lily and Arin."

"No"

"What?" I stop and ask him.

"I have a set, you have a set and your brother gets a set. Nobody else."

"Why?"

"Because people lose keys all the time, and I do not know them. Therefore; I do not trust them. Tell me about Lilly and Arin."

"Well Lily came to me about six months after the Inker's expo. She was working for a sexist pig at a shop in Sacramento. She's been with me ever since. Arin is a local; she graduated high school last year and has been taking art classes at the community college."

"This Lily chick, she just ups and moves, following you around like a lost puppy?"

I completely lose it and get in his face. "Lily is my ride or die! She is an adult female with no family and nothing tying her down. She can do whatever she damn well pleases. And just so you know, so can I!"

Baratta

Damn that fire in her eyes when she's standing up for her friend makes my cock, hard as a steel pole. Once she gets the door unlocked and goes into the shop I get my laptop out of the car. I plan to do some research while she works.

She has a sitting area with a table and couch for people waiting. I choose that as my work space. I find it interesting that Lily followed her from New Orleans, so I have to find out more about this woman.

I start at the Inker's expo Facebook page and dive into the pictures from when Fiona was there. Almost every picture of Fi has either Lily or some guy in them.

The guy looks slightly familiar but his features seem to be distorted somehow. "Hey Fiona." I call out and she pops her head up from where she is inking Wrench.

"A little busy here."

"I just need a minute. Bet Wrench could use a break."

"No, I'm good", he calls out but I repeat myself.

"I bet Wrench could use a break."

"Yeah, I'm going to smoke Fiona." He finally picks up on my tone of voice.

She stomps over to me. "You can't interfere with my work, this is my livelihood."

"Like I said, I have a question." I point to the pictures. "Who is this man? He is in almost every picture from New Orleans."

She finally looks down at my laptop. "Oh that is Clint."

"And who is Clint? What is he to you?"

"He is just a wannabe. His work is shit. I can draw better than him with my eyes closed. But, he is a nice guy. He has been trying to get me to hire him for the last two years.

I tried to let him down gently when he applied here. I think he finally got the message because he hasn't contacted me since his interview."

Just then Wrench walks back in, so she has to go back to work. Now I have two suspects to research. I still haven't told Fi about the batch of pictures that came yesterday, but now I know it has something to do with New Orleans, so I'm going to focus there.

She finishes up with Wrench and has a couple more club members to work on. Lily is busy doing a memorial tattoo for a local woman that lost her son in a car accident, while Arin is practicing on grapefruits.

I spend the next few hours searching through Lily and Clint's background. I find nothing connecting the two except the expo. They aren't even from the same part of the country.

I print off a picture of Clint grabbing it off the printer before anyone sees it. Then send pictures of both of them to my contacts. I have basic research skills, but Buzz is better.

Buzz from the New Orleans Night Howler's chapter can find information on anyone, anywhere and he does not ask questions. We are in different time zones, so I don't expect an answer tonight.

I shut down my gear, then stretch. I can feel every bone in my body cracking from sitting so long. I'm an action man; I'm not used to doing the research myself. Stretching my legs I wander over to Fiona's workstation, she's tatting a man I've seen around the club but don't know.

"Hey beautiful." I call out; I don't want to make her jump while she's working.

"I'm almost done here, just got some shading left."

"Lily and Arin are done for the night. I'm going to walk them out. Wait here for me." I plan to take the chance to ask Lily some questions, while I walk her to her car.

"So Lily, how did you end up working for Fiona?"

"I met her in New Orleans two years ago. I was working for a pig. Asshole was always grabbing my tits or my ass, thinking it was funny. Then one night I forgot my purse in the shop, when I went back for it I overheard him on the phone telling someone how he was going to 'tap that' if I wanted it or not. I got the hell out of there."

"But why Fiona? There are thousands of tattoo parlors in California. You could have found work anywhere."

"I didn't want to work for a man, and Fiona is the best. Working for her, gets me seen. Besides, at the convention, Fi told me her dream was always to open a shop made up entirely of kickass women. The only grabby hands I have to deal with while working for her are customers and I can always tattoo a dick on them if they can't keep their hands to themselves."

I can not hold back my laugh, "Shit you are as mean as Fi." she just shrugs her shoulders.

"I learned from the best."

"You should join the self defense class." I suggest.

"Arin and I are signed up to start next week. Fi requires it as part of our employment, she even pays for us." With that she closes her car door and drives away.

Fiona

When Baratta returns I thank him for walking the girls out and lock up. It has been a long day and I'm exhausted. You would think my job is easy but crouching down over another person for hours can wear a person out.

He starts to say something but I just hold my hand up to stop him. "I'm tired and I'm hungry. I just want to heat something up and go to sleep. Please hold it until morning."

"Tomorrow is Saturday and I know you are closed. I just want to know your plans."

"I'm meeting my brother at the shooting range at 9 then we have the family BBQ the rest of the day."

He takes my hand, together we walk out the back door. I stop to lock the door but he says, "I got this, I'll be right behind you."

As I'm zombie walking towards the stairs, I hear a noise. My head snaps up and I'm suddenly alert. It sounds like crying or whimpering and it's coming from behind the dumpster.

Since Baratta installed the security lights, it is much brighter back here. I pull the dumpster away from the wall and wiggle behind it.

Baratta is shouting at me, "What are you doing? Get out of there." But I'm determined.

"I heard something."

I'm frantically looking and I'm about to give up when I hear it again. I follow the sound and to my surprise I find a puppy. It's clinging to the side of the building like it's looking for warmth. The poor thing is dirty and clearly hasn't had a good meal in a long time.

I scoop him up, then turn and hold him out for Baratta to take so I can get out of here. "Take him."

"I'm not touching that. You don't know where it has been." He holds his hands up as he backs away.

"Well I'm not leaving it out here to die."

He reluctantly takes the puppy from me, while we go up the stairs. I take a quick look around to see if there are any surprises by the door before unlocking it.

Kicking my shoes off, I let out a sigh of relief before taking the puppy back. "I'm going to shower and give this little guy a bath. Will you please heat up something for us to eat? There are storage bowls in the freezer from Sunshine, they're labeled. Just pick something; I'm too tired to be picky tonight."

"What are you going to do with that thing?" He asks, pointing to the pup.

"Tonight I'm going to clean it up and feed it. I'll decide tomorrow what to do for the long term."

I don't take long in the shower. I'm in my robe and the pup is wrapped in a towel when I go back out to the kitchen. Baratta has two plates set out; it looks like rice with some kind of stir fry. I don't care. With the puppy in one hand I'm scooping up food in the other.

"Give me the puppy so you can eat."

I hand him over and notice Baratta has put a bowl of food and a bowl of water on the floor. He puts the pup down before joining me at the table. "Thank you."

The next few minutes the only sound that can be heard is the scrape of our forks on our plates and pup chowing down.

The silence is broken by Baratta, "You know he is going to shit in about thirty minutes if not sooner? Where is it going to sleep?"

"Can you go back down to the shop? In the storage room is a pet crate. I keep it for clients that bring pets with them."

"Lock the door behind me."

"But you are only going to be gone for a few minutes."

"Fiona, please just lock the door behind me."

Baratta

I'm about halfway down the stairs when I hear the crunch of footsteps on gravel. I move closer to the side of the building, crouching down to make myself smaller. I can't make out any specific features but the person is lean and short. Wearing dark pants and a hoodie.

He or she has an envelope in their hands. I decide it must be a man because as he gets closer I can see a hint of facial hair. When he gets to the bottom of the stairs, I pop up like a jack in the box hoping to catch him off guard. But; the little fucker is quick and I'm still on the stairway. He drops the package he was carrying as he sprints away.

"Fuck!" I yell as I turn and punch the side of the building. I can't go after him because that would leave Fi unprotected. I pick up the envelope he dropped and slide it into the back of my pants, then go get the dog crate like Fiona asked me to.

When I get back upstairs, Fiona is sitting on the couch with the puppy curled up in her lap. The instant she sees my bloody hand, she demands an explanation. "What happened to you?"

"I tripped on the steps."

"And bloodied your knuckles?" She looks at me in disbelief. "Come on let's get you cleaned up."

She takes my bloody hand and pulls me over to the sink, running cold water over it.

While she is focused on the blood I slip my other hand behind my back, pulling out the envelope, I slid it behind the coffee maker. I'm not hiding it from her forever; I just want to look at it before she sees it.

After wrapping my hand in a towel, she gets an ice pack from the freezer and hands it to me. "Hold this on your knuckles for a few minutes, and then I will wrap it for you."

I'm sitting at the table with the ice pack while she goes to the bathroom for her first aid kit. Before I know it, She has my hand wrapped and is handing me a couple pain pills with a glass of water. I'm a little stunned at her reaction; no one has ever looked out for me before.

Aunt Morgania would have fussed over me but she is family, it's not the same thing. The women I've been with in the past might have wrapped my hand but only so I would not get blood on them. Fiona actually cares, I can tell by the gentle way she took care of my injury.

She puts the puppy in the crate before coming back for me. Taking my uninjured hand she walks with me to the bedroom. Slipping out of her robe, she slides under the covers. "Are you coming?" I have a little trouble getting my jeans undone one handed but after struggling for a few minutes I get them off.

Once I'm in the bed, Fiona turns her back to me and snuggles closer. I can feel her heat on my dick, but it is also obvious tonight is going to be for sleeping. She reaches back, grabbing my arm and pulling it around her. "Just hold me," She mumbles before drifting off to sleep.

Fiona

I wake up snuggled in Baratta's arms. I want to stay here, where I'm warm and comfortable but the puppy we found last night is whimpering, needing to go to the bathroom. I also have to meet my brother at the gun range …

"OH SHIT" I scramble to get up. I'm late. "Blood is going to kill me. Baratta! BARATTA! I gotta go." I'm trying to put my pants and shirt on quickly but I get tangled up in my clothes causing me to fall on my ass.

Speaking of my ass, Baratta is sitting on the bed laughing at me. Wait a minute, did I call Baratta mine?

I'm furiously trying to finish getting dressed before I scoop the puppy out of the crate and grab my keys while running for the door. I'm almost out the door when Baratta snags me around the waist.

"Slow down Mario"

"I can't, you don't understand. Blood has been way overprotective since I got back. He's not going to back off unless he sees for himself that I can protect myself. I need him to back off, for my sanity. I have to go."

"Why are you taking the puppy?"

"I will ask one of the Prospects to get him some food and the kids can play with him for a bit. I don't really have anything here for him, he can't keep eating people food and I can't leave him in the crate all day."

"I have a few things to do in town this morning and I have a feeling you won't hear from your stalker today. Go ahead without me and I'll meet you at the clubhouse at noon." He says before planting a kiss on me.

I'm halfway down the steps when he calls out, "Got your gun?"

I turn running back up the stairs but he stops me at the door and holds it out for me. With another kiss, I'm finally on my way.

I think I ran all three red lights in this town, thankfully there wasn't much traffic. Finally, I pull up to the clubhouse and I'm only ten minutes late. I sit in my car for a minute to just breathe as I look over at the puppy.

He sat in the seat like a gentleman, behaving perfectly the whole way here.

"You need a name before I take you in there." I reach out, pulling him into my lap. "Toby? No. Magnum is a strong manly name. No. Winchester? No. I got it! Since you have that beautiful blue coat why don't I just call you Blue, but with a French twist to make you more sophisticated. Your name is Bleu! Do you like that?"

Poor puppy must think I'm crazy for talking to him like this. I shake my head, time to face the music. I take Bleu to the clubhouse and deliver him to the kids' playroom. "Mina, Mina, Mina." I sing out. "I have a new baby for you to spoil." She gives me an odd look before I reveal the puppy.

"Mina meet Bleu, Bleu meet your Auntie Mina. Baratta and I found him last night." She's still giving me crazy eyes, when the kids see Bleu and choruses of "Puppy, puppy" ring through the room.

"Mina, I have to get out to the range or Blood is going to kick my ass. I'm already late. Can one of the prospects go get him some puppy food? Please and thank you," I say running out the door.

"Bear" I call one of the members, "Can you please grab a buggy and escort me out to the range."

Ever since the girls and I tortured that dickhead with frogs in the box, we have to be escorted every time we go out to the back of the property.

Bear calls ahead on his two way, making sure I'm expected. He doesn't want to have trouble with the boss if I was pulling one over on him. Geez, you drug one little Prospect and nobody trusts you anymore.

Chapter 5
Baratta

After leaving Fiona's, I head to the pet store that's on the other side of town. Her new puppy will need all kinds of things. They are a lot of work to take care of just like little babies.

I like kids well enough but I'm not too sure I would make a good dad. It's a lot of responsibility that I'm not too sure I want in my life. To care like that for another human? It takes guts. Especially one that is completely dependent upon you.

After finding the aisle with all the puppy food, it took me nearly half an hour to make a selection. There are so many to choose from and I wanted to be sure I picked the one that is most nutritious.

Just from looking at him, I can tell he is going to be a big dog, so I pick out not only a bed that will fit him now but I pick one up that is a bit bigger as well.

I find the aisle with all the collars as well as leashes. I get several different sizes for the one that has spikes. Fiona I think will love them.

After making all of my selections, I head to the register but get side tracked when I pass by a toy section. Puppies like to chew right? So how could I possibly pass by all of that without getting toys?

"You must have quite a few dogs." The cashier comments as she rings up my purchases.

"Just one." I murmur.

She doesn't say anything else but her eyes seemed to get big at the idea of buying so much for one dog. Its shit he'll need, so I don't know why that would raise eyebrows.

I just get back to Fiona's apartment when my phone rings. Looking down I can see that it is Buzz calling from New Orleans. Hoping he has something for me, I answer it.

"I'm assuming you got some information for me?" I say as soon as I answer.

"Hello to you too Jackass."

"What is it, Buzzy? Is my cousin still ignoring you?"

"Don't call me Buzzy you fucker! And yes, she's still ignoring me. I didn't call to chit chat with you about your cousin. I got something on the guy in the picture you sent."

"What did you find?" He has my full attention now by his tone of voice.

"I ran the name I found from the Expo and came up with nothing so I ran his picture through some facial recognition software. It got a hit but when I tried to open the file, it threw up a brick wall. I sent it over to a contact of mine within the FBI. I'm emailing you everything he sent back. You're not going to believe what's in these files man."

"How bad is this threat to Fiona?"

"That's just it. I know this guy and Fiona met during the expo but I don't think he was there for her. I think he was tracking you."

"Fuck."

"Yeah, fuck. I know your skill set so this is probably going to go in one ear and out the other but if you need me there, I'm one call away."

"I appreciate it but for now I think I have it under control."

"Well the offer still stands. I'll keep trying to track his movements from here but I don't know how much good it will do. He's had the same training as you although he didn't excel at it like you did. However, I think he's a little more blood thirsty."

"What's the name in his file?"

"Harold Cache. Also known as the Mad Dog."

The name causes me to go completely still. I've more than heard of him. I know him very well. How did I not recognize him? He must have done something to his face.

We had gotten word through intelligence that he was working with other cartels that wanted to eliminate the competition. They were eliminating them alright, even the women and children.

The things he did to them came straight out of nightmares. In this business you still have to have a code. No women and no children.

Fiona

"Told you I could still out shoot your ass." I smile smugly at my brother.

"Well I'm glad to know that being so famous hasn't made you lose all your sense. Can't say the same for your choice in men though." He grumbles.

"My sex life is none of your business."

"I don't want to know about your sex life." He curls his nose in disgust.

"Then what is your problem?" I huff out as I roll my eyes.

"Baratta is just not someone you should get mixed up with is all I'm saying. You don't really know him."

"And you do?" I roll my eyes again. "I may not know everything about him. Yet. But what I do know is that he is kind and protective. You are going to have to step back and let me live my own life."

"I just want to keep you from getting hurt."

"I know that but you tend to forget that I am more like you than you would have others to believe. After all, red is my favorite color." I widen my eyes while looking directly into his.

"I haven't forgotten half pint."

"I thought about going up there. To the mountain. Just to see if they rotted the ground."

"They haven't."

"You've been up there? When?" I ask with surprise.

"About two years ago. I'd heard they were building some cabins in the area. I wanted to be sure one wasn't built there. So I went to check, and then bought the twenty acres. I went back again and planted a fig tree directly over the spot. That way each year rotting figs litter that exact spot." He smiles at the thought while I giggle.

"Ruthless brother dear. Just ruthless." We both just sit and laugh while drinking a beer.

Today was a great day that I truly enjoyed. I've missed my brother while being away. Hopefully we don't miss so many of these chances to hang out again.

I walk into the apartment with the puppy in my arms and there are bags of stuff sitting everywhere. One look tells me that Baratta apparently bought out the pet supply store.

"Have fun with your brother?" He asks as he walks out of the bedroom.

"I kicked his ass as usual. Why didn't you come to the BBQ? Everyone was expecting you." I was expecting him but I leave that part out.

"I had to get caught up on some work after going to the pet supply store."

"Did you leave anything at the store?" I say as I look around yet again at all of the bags.

"What do you mean? He is going to need all of this." Surprise is evident on his face telling me that he is completely serious.

"He's not going to need that huge bed for several months. Do you really think he needed five bags of dog food?"

"Just wanted to be sure he had plenty in case there was a shortage." He tries to hold a serious expression but it doesn't last long when we both start to laugh.

"I've got his bath ready so I'll get him all washed up with this amazing dog soap I got while you relax a bit." He holds his arms out until I hand over the puppy.

"Actually, I'm a little hungry. I thought I'd call in a delivery from that Chinese restaurant down the road."

"Sounds great. But didn't you eat at the BBQ?"

"No. I was too busy waiting for you."

"I'm sorry; I should have been there for you. Go ahead and place the order while I take care of this little guy."

I watch as he heads to the bathroom to give Bleu a bath. I can't help but shake my head at him. He acts as if having the dog is a hindrance but I can tell from the amount of stuff he bought for him that he loves the puppy. Good thing because I love the puppy already and don't plan to give him up.

After calling in our order, I head to the kitchen to get plates and drinks ready. While standing at the counter, I see something behind the coffee maker. Grabbing it, I see it's an envelope like the ones from before.

I'm just looking through its contents when Baratta comes into the kitchen. He stiffens when he sees what I have in my hands.

"When did these come?" I look directly at him waiting for an answer.

"Last night." He murmurs. I realize that when something is going on or he doesn't really want to answer, his voice gets a little bit quieter.

"Last night? Why did you not tell me? Why the hell are they hidden behind the coffee pot?" My voice gets a little louder with each question.

"I wasn't hiding them. I just wanted time to process the information. Possibly reach out to some of my contacts and see what we could come up with. Those aren't the only ones." I say as I go get the ones that were here while she was kickboxing with Austin at the gym.

"You had no right! You should have told me as soon as you got them! And in a way, that is technically hiding them!"

There's a knock on the door as soon as I finish talking.

"Pay for the food. I'm going to take a shower." I say through gritted teeth before I stomp down the hallway.

I climb under the spray of the water hoping it will wash away some of the anger I'm currently feeling. I realize he is just trying to help but it reminds me of my brother always trying to take control. And that just pisses me off.

I'm just standing under the spray while the hot water beats down on my back when I hear the glass door to the shower open. I don't bother turning around as I know that it's Baratta.

"I'm sorry." He whispers in my ear as he presses his naked length to my back.

Even pissed off at him, my body still reacts to his closeness. His hands slowly glide down my sides over the curve of my hips. Unable to control myself, I push my ass back into him.

"Will you forgive me?" He whispers again as he pushes back into me.

"You can't do that. You can't take control like that. I don't like it. I expect to be your equal and I'm not just a helpless woman."

"I just want to protect you." His voice is sincere.

Turning to face him, I look up into his eyes.

"I get that Baratta but I'm not an innocent angel. You have no idea what I am capable of." I whisper back before laying my head on his shoulder wondering what he would think of me if I ever told him the truth of what I had done. What my brother and the MC covered up to protect me.

"I know we don't know everything about each other completely, yet. But I've seen the fire in your eyes. It's the same fire I've seen in your brother's eyes." He lifts my head until I'm looking back at him.

I feel as though I could tell him anything and it would still all be okay. The weird part though that I'm still not sure he would be okay with is the fact I don't feel the least bit guilty about what I did. I even catch myself smiling when I think about it. Just like my brother did earlier today.

I'm brought back to the moment from my thoughts when I feel Baratta's hands slowly moving over the curve of my ass cheeks. Lifting me up, I wrap my legs around his waist putting my core directly against his cock. I can't stop the sigh that escapes my lips at the heat radiating off of him.

He lifts me up and down gliding himself between my already wet pussy coating himself with my essence.

"Oh, God, that feels so good. Do you feel what you do to me, woman?" His voice sounding strained as he continues to torture us both.

He lifts me up a little higher to line himself up with my entrance. He grabs my right nipple with his mouth, biting down slightly as he eases me slowly down onto his hardness filling me up.

He sets a hard pace hitting my clit with his pelvic bone every time he slams into me, never letting go of my nipple with his mouth, only sucking on it harder in a throbbing rhythm that can be felt deep within my core.

I'm so close to the edge and ready to let go but feeling as if I need just a little bit more.

"Come for me Fi, come for me now!" He grits out after letting my nipple go with a pop. One more hard slam into my pussy sends me over the edge as I scream from the pleasure that I am learning only he can give to me.

Chapter 6
Baratta

It's been a long day for Fiona, I wore her out. I am laying in bed watching her sleep when my phone sends out an alert. I know that sound intimately; I was praying not to hear it for a while longer. It means I have a job to do.

As gently as possible I wake her up. "Fiona, Fi."

"I can't Bar, I got nothing left."

At first I want to laugh that she thinks I am waking her up for sex but then I realize she has given me a nickname. Some of my contacts call me Ghost because of my job, but no one has ever given me a nickname before.

"My love, I have to go to work."

She is suddenly awake. "But I thought Tony knew why you were here, why would he call you away?"

"Not Tony, my other job."

"Huh?" she says while rubbing the sleep out of her eyes.

"It's my government job, I am on-call. When they call I have to go. I don't get a choice."

"What do you do?"

"I can't tell you, it's classified. I'll probably be gone for about a week."

She is so beautiful when she is half asleep like this, I want to climb back in the bed but duty calls. Fiona grabs my pillow from where I was sleeping just a few minutes ago, wrapping her arms around it. "Be safe"

Grabbing my go bag from her closet, I stop at the door, calling back to her "Take care of my dog while I am gone."

She jumps up in the bed, "Bleu is my dog." I just laugh as I duck away from the pillow she has thrown at me.

"Call your brother. Tell him about the pictures, please." I can still hear her mumbling as I get to the door.

Fiona

Baratta has been gone for five days. The morning after he left, it felt strange to wake up alone. That is when I knew my feelings for him are real. I have never missed having a man in my bed before. I haven't heard from him this whole time either. No text, no calls, nothing. I'm starting to get worried.

It has been an unusual five days. One of my celebrity clients snuck into town for some work, so I had to close the shop to the public. Lily has been more jumpy than usual, plus I keep seeing Wolfsbane club members everywhere I go.

The strangest thing though is that I haven't got any pictures from my mysterious photographer the whole time. Is it weird that while Baratta was here I received pictures almost every day but now that he's gone they've stopped?

Since I couldn't open to the public while my celebrity guest was here, I was able to close up early tonight.

I'm sitting on the floor in my living room playing tug with Bleu when I hear someone stumbling up the stairs to my apartment. I know it isn't my brother, he would've called first and Baratta never makes noise. He's like a damn ghost.

Grabbing my gun I quickly deposit Bleu into his crate. Crouching down behind the sofa, I have my gun aimed at the door when I hear a key in the lock.

Moments later Baratta staggers in. He has blood running down the side of his face. I put the safety back on the gun and drop it on the couch before rushing over to him.

Upon seeing me, he says "Fiona" then topples over. I can't catch him because he's so much bigger than me but I throw my weight against him to slow his fall. After lowering him to the floor, I lock the door and run for the first aid kit.

I check his body over for injuries but the only one I can find is a gash on his head, so I clean it up. I'm dabbing at it with rubbing alcohol when Baratta starts mumbling. The only words I can understand are airport, car, crash and Fiona.

I shush him so I can focus on the gash. It's really deep; he's certainly going to need stitches. I don't have anything to numb it with but I can do the stitches myself. Growing up in my family, I learned how to do them. It was either that or spend hours in the E.R. with my brother.

Not wanting to get lost in thoughts of the Step Monster I clear my head, and then get to work. It's a good thing he is passed out or this would hurt like a bitch.

Knowing I can't move him by myself, plus he wouldn't want me to call anyone, I cover him with a blanket. I get out some pain killers with a glass of water, leaving them on the coffee table.

Grabbing my own blanket off my bed, I get comfortable on the couch so I can watch over him until he wakes up.

After a couple hours I must have fallen asleep because I feel myself being lifted and carried to my bed. Once he lays me down, he climbs in next to me.

"I missed you." I say before I go back to sleep snuggled up next to him.

When I wake up the next morning, Baratta is sitting on the side of the bed, his elbows on his knees and his head in his hands.

"Who did you call?" He asks me.

74

"What do you mean by that? I didn't call anyone." He gives me a blank look, almost like he doesn't believe me.

"If you didn't call anyone, then who stitched me up?"

"I did!" Now I am getting mad. "Maybe I should have left you there to bleed!"

I head for the bathroom mumbling to myself. "Ungrateful bastard." When I come out, he's waiting for me.

"I'm sorry; I didn't know you could do that."

"I'm sorry too; I keep forgetting you haven't known me very long. Some days, it just feels like you have always been part of my life. Can you tell me what happened?"

"Can we please have some coffee first, along with something for my pounding head?"

We go out to the kitchen and I tell him to sit down while I make the coffee. I grab him some meds, handing them to him for him to take. After I fix his coffee, I wait for him to begin.

"The job went well, easy in and out. I stopped off in New Orleans to update Tony and pick up my bike."

"You ride?" I interrupted him.

"Yes, I'm not in a club or anything like that, I just like the freedom my bike gives me sometimes."

"I would like to ride with you."

"I can arrange that." He says, "But let me get back to what happened. The plane landed around 10 last night and since I didn't have to wait for a car, I jumped right on my bike and headed here. I was about a mile out of town, when a car came out of nowhere. The shoulder of the road was too steep for me to move over; it just plowed over me and took off."

"Wait a minute. You brought a motorcycle on a plane?" I ask.

"When your family owns the plane you can load anything you want in the cargo section."

He gets up to refill his coffee, while I grab my phone. "Who are you calling?"

"I'm just going to call my brother. You said your bike is about a mile out?"

"Yeah you know that last intersection before the city limits? That is where the car pulled out behind me."

"I promise I won't tell him anything. I'm only going to ask him to get your bike and bring it back here."

"Thank you", he sighs as he sits back down. "I stayed to take care of you, but here you are taking care of me."

I make the call then wrestle Baratta back to bed. "Please rest. Only your head got cracked open but I am sure your body hurts."

"Yeah it feels like I got hit by a car." He jokes.

"Too soon?" He asks with a smirk as I groan.

"Definitely too soon, now rest." I feel his forehead around the wound. Checking to make sure it doesn't feel hot or show any signs of infection, then slip out of the room.

I'm at the kitchen table sketching when Bleu starts whining. Putting him on the leash, I make sure I have my keys and my gun is tucked into its holster under my jacket.

When Bleu and I step outside, by the door is another envelope. "God Damnit!" I shout as I throw it inside. I don't even care where it landed; I just want to take my dog for a friggin walk. Slamming the door, I continue on my way.

In the week since we found Bleu. Being cared for, being provided with a constant source of food and water has turned my raggedy little dumpster puppy into a handsome, happy puppy.

He practically drags me as we walk down the block to the park. This park is great; there is a little fenced area for pets. There's nobody else here, so I let Bleu off his leash to let him just run and play for about thirty minutes.

I'm sitting on a bench when I see the Wolfsbane tow truck drive past. So I call Bleu and head back to my building.

Blood is unloading the bike when I get back. I don't want to get in his way so I head up. "Hey bro, come up when you're done." Stopping me at the bottom of the steps, he hands me something.

Looking down I see that it's Baratta's helmet. The face shield is shattered and the helmet is cracked. "Oh My God" I mutter as I lower myself to sit on the steps. Turning it over the inside is soaked in blood. "How did he walk away from that?" My brother takes me by the hand and pulls me upstairs.

I am putting Bleu in his crate, when Blood suddenly shouts, "WHAT THE FUCK IS THIS!!" When I turn around he's holding the envelope in one hand and a picture of me in the other.

"Oh shit"

"Oh shit? Is that all you have to say?"

"Calm down, Baratta is sleeping."

"Calm down! Calm down! I will not calm down." If anything he is getting louder. "How long has this been going on?"

"Blood sit down, have a cup of coffee, I will tell you everything but not if you keep screaming at me."

"I don't want coffee! You got a beer?"

"Yes just sit down and let me get it for you."

When I bring his beer back, he's sitting in the same position I found Baratta in this morning; Elbows on his knees, hands in his hair. It must be a man thing, I think to myself. I sit next to him but he doesn't say anything. He just drinks his beer.

I can tell he's calming himself so I just sit there in silence waiting for him to start the conversation. He doesn't take long.

"How long has this been going on?"

"Since opening day."

"Does HE know?"

"Yes, he was here when they arrived."

"Why didn't either of you tell me?"

"Because I didn't want you to know."

"Why? I can protect you."

"That is why." He gives me a confused look, "I can protect myself, Blood. I proved it when I took out our Step Monster along with our shitty ass mother."

"You shouldn't have had to do that by yourself. I should have been there." He pulls me into a hug. "I should have done it, not you. I should have been there to protect you."

"Taking a life brings darkness into your soul. The darkness grows with each life you take." a voice says from the hallway.

We both look and ask, "What?" at the same time.

Baratta laughs, "You are definitely siblings."

He walks the rest of the way into the room, sitting down in a chair. "What is happening?"

I look from my brother to Baratta. "Blood found some pictures."

"I asked you to tell him."

"I was planning on it; I didn't want him to find out this way."

Blood interrupts our stare down, "Baratta, why didn't you tell me someone is after my sister?"

"She begged me not to, besides he isn't after her. He's after me."

"What?" we both say at the same time again. My jaw is hanging open, I don't know what to say, but Blood has plenty to say.

"What have you dragged my sister into?"

"I haven't dragged her into anything. He's been tracking her for two years. He wants to take me out, but I think he has other plans for Fiona."

Chapter 7
Baratta

Fi and Blood look like I just dropped a bomb on them. I guess I did. Between the assignment and the accident I haven't had a chance to tell Fiona everything I found out. Now I have to share the information with her brother too. Meanwhile my head is pounding like someone is running a jackhammer against it.

"Fi, can I please have more painkillers? I was going to get them myself but I don't know where you keep them. I will tell you everything I found out. I just need to stop the pounding in my head."

When Fi comes back with two tablets and a glass of water I chug them down. Blood hasn't moved his eyes off of me since I entered the room. I decide to ignore him.

"This morning, I told you I stopped in New Orleans to pick up my bike. While I was there, one of my local contacts sent me a bunch of information.

So I checked it out. Included in that info was an address for an apartment in the French Quarter. When I got there, no one was around so I broke in.

The apartment had a dark room. I found pictures of you and me. The pictures of you had hearts and flowers doodled all over them. The pictures of me had targets drawn over my head. My eyes crossed out, there were even slash marks drawn across my throat."

I leave them to digest the information, heading back to Fiona's bed. A wave of dizziness washes through me but I take a moment to get my balance back. Fiona notices but I wave her away when she starts to follow.

"Stay, I got this. I'm going to lie down before I fall over again."

"Who is he, Baratta? Who is after you?"

"You know him as Clint, but that isn't his real name." With those parting words, I exit the room.

Fiona

"No, no way Clint?" I can't believe it. Sweet wannabe Clint. The guy who thinks he is a world class artist but can't draw his way out of a paper bag. I am stunned into silence.

Blood doesn't let the silence last long. He snaps me out of it by asking, "Who is Clint?"

"I met him at the expo in New Orleans, two years ago. He said he was a tattoo artist but I didn't see any of his work, until recently. He has stayed in contact with me. When I put out the call for employees, I couldn't say I wanted all women it would have been discrimination. I had to accept apps from anyone that wanted to apply. I even called a few men in for interviews. He was one of them."

"I need another beer for this." Blood interrupts me, getting up to get it himself. I think he wants to give me a minute, my brother knows me. While he's gone my phone rings.

Looking at the screen, I see the call is from Hay's Den. I almost hit the ignore button but then I remember I was supposed to have a class today, so I answer it. "I am sorry Austin but I can't kick your ass today. Something has come up. I'll call you later."

When I hang up Blood, sits down. "Alright sis, I gave you a few minutes for everything to sink in. Now tell me the rest."

"Remember when I was doing interviews last month? I had a bunch of grapefruits; you all thought I lost my mind. I asked the interviewees to draw any picture they wanted and tat the fruit so I could evaluate their skills.

I never did figure out what Clint's design was supposed to be. He claimed it was some kind of tribal peace symbol but it looked more like a poop emoji. Trust me, Blood it was so bad I almost laughed in his face. I felt bad for him, so I asked him to do another one.

Maybe he was having a bad day. This time I asked him to draw a turtle, sitting on a log. I thought maybe he is better with more direction. Nope, I had to keep a straight face when he showed me a blob on a stick."

I reach for my cell phone, opening the gallery and I bring up the pictures of his contributions.

"Blood, I swear I laughed for two days. I was laughing so hard I had tears streaming from my eyes."

"I bet you let him down gently, too."

"You have no idea how hard it was for me to tell him I would keep him on file as a backup artist. The minute he walked out the door, I was rolling on the floor."

"You know I have to tell the club about this." Suddenly serious, Blood tells me.

"Please don't, Baratta has more information now. He can catch this guy."

"I will give you a week, but I can't keep this from Timber for long. What if it puts the people of our town in danger? Do you have a picture of this guy? I can at least make sure he isn't renting a club owned cabin."

"Thank you; you are my favorite big brother." I say as I throw my arms around him for a hug.

"I am your only big brother." He responds to our old joke. "I guess you are keeping the prick?"

"As long as he'll let me." is my answer.

Before he walks out the door he tells me that he will take Baratta's bike to the shop and have the guys fix it up for him. He can't have his brother-in-law riding a piece of shit.

I grab something to eat and play with Bleu for a little bit, then check on Baratta one more time before heading down to Poison Pen. Since today is the first day I'll be open to the public this week, I expect it to be busy, I am not wrong.

Baratta came down a couple of times to check on me. The stairs were hard on him; I had to help him back up them each time. I finally had to put my foot down.

"If you come down those steps one more time tonight, I am going to leave you on the couch in the shop."

"But I need to keep you safe."

"Right now you are more of a hindrance than a help. Please just stay up here and let me do my work." I tell him as I tuck him back into bed. He reaches up, pushing my hair out of my face. "You never have to work another day in your life, if you don't want to."

"But I want to," I whisper, exiting the room. I know it is his injured brain talking. Surely, He knows me better than that by now. I stop to make sure Bleu has fresh food and water before returning to the client sitting in my chair.

The next two days fly by quickly and quietly. Between working, taking care of Baratta and my fitness class. I'm exhausted, falling into bed at the end of each day. The pictures still come but I ignore them. Blood called to check if I was going to attend the family BBQ, but even that was too much.

Baratta was getting better each day but I noticed he still had some dizzy spells. When he thought I wasn't looking his face would scrunch up in pain. I didn't dare ask how he was feeling; I remember how big of a baby my brother is anytime he gets hurt.

By Sunday afternoon, I'm at my wits end. So I call Miranda to arrange some time out. I don't know if Baratta will hang with the guys or just stay in but I have to get away from him. He walks in just as I'm getting off the phone with her.

"You know the entire time you were gone, I couldn't wait for you to get back. I love you but I need a break. Just a few hours with the girls."

"You love me?"

"Yes I love you, but you are a big baby when you are hurt."

He repeats his question, "You love me?"

"Well isn't it obvious? I was mad when I thought you left me in New Orleans, I cried when you came here, I missed you when you were gone and I took care of you when you were hurt. I LOVE YOU. Do I need to clarify it more? You want me to tattoo it on my ass?"

"Well" he says thoughtfully, "If you tattoo it on your ass, I can see it every time you bend over for me."

"If I tattoo it on my ass, then I get to put 'Property of Fiona' on your cock." I walk away laughing but I could swear I hear him say, "Bring it baby."

I turn back to get the last word. "I can't tat my own ass. I would have to get someone else to do it."

I should've known he would have a follow up. "That's ok I trust that Lily isn't into you."

Shaking my head I leave the room. We could go back and forth like this for hours, while it would be entertaining; I just made plans with my sister-in-law. She is going to gather up the girls and meet me at Bella's Brew.

I was going to suggest we go to a local dive bar, but that wouldn't be fair to Miranda or Mina since they can't drink.

On my way out the door, I remember something that was bothering me and turn back. "Hey Baratta, while you were gone for work. I noticed some of the club guys hanging around. I know you didn't rat me out to my brother. Any idea what's up with that?"

"I called Timber on my way out of town to let him know I'd be gone for a few days. Maybe he sent them around."

"You going to join the club?"

"No, I thought about it, but Timber said I would have to go in as a prospect. There is no way I'm going to be a grunt at this point in my life."

"Ok, I heard they were considering taking on some new prospects. See ya." I walk to the door once again.

"Get back here woman."

"Excuse me?"

"Damn, I think your head just did a 360. Like in that exorcist movie. Come here and kiss me."

Baratta

Fiona is right; I have been a bear the last few days. I'm a little surprised she put up with my shit. Blood came by yesterday while she was working and showed me my helmet. Not even I can believe I walked away from that.

I remember hearing the car rev up behind me, then waking up on her floor with stitches in my head. I have no clue how I got from the accident site to her apartment.

Remembering that Blood wanted all the details and to see the pictures. I decide to call him over while the girls are doing their thing.

When he gets here, I show him everything I've got. I pull them from their hiding place, I'm about to hand them to him but stop myself.

"You want me to pull out the naked pictures? I don't imagine you want to see your sister that way."

"There are naked pictures?"

"Yeah, man the first one that was delivered was a shot of her in the shower. That's why she keeps the curtains closed now."

We talk while he looks through the pics. I point out the ones that I knew the time or location of. I can't put the Seattle pics in the timeline because I wasn't part of her life then.

After going through the stack he let out a breath. "This is bullshit, why is this guy fixated on my sister."

"From what I've put together, he met her before I did. Those first expo pics, I didn't meet her until the expo was over. It was the last night; she was at a club with Lily and a few others. I originally thought Clint was there with her group, but now I am thinking he was watching me.

I was there looking out for Mr. Marcus. When his meeting ended I stayed with Fi. We hung out the rest of the night. Then in the morning we got separated by a stupid misunderstanding."

"What kind of misunderstanding keeps people apart for two years?"

"I went out to get us coffee, but didn't leave a note. Couldn't find a damn pen, you would think a hotel room would have a pen. I didn't want to wake her. When she woke up to find me gone, she packed her shit and ran for the airport. I got back to find her gone. I thought she didn't want me. I didn't know her last name, her flight numbers; I didn't even know where she called home."

"Man that sucks, my sister is special but she has been through hell. I'm going to give you a hard time though. I have to; it's a big bro code. As long as you take care of her, I won't interfere. Just keep in mind you hurt her and you are a dead man."

"I swear on my life. When she walked into that clubhouse, everything changed."

"Timber mentioned to you about being part of the club?"

"Nah, thought about it for a minute but I'm nobody's grunt. That is what I would be if I prospected."

"He told me you said that, so we had a different idea."

"I'm listening."

"What if we list you as a consultant? That would give you access to the club and club events, like the family barbecue. You wouldn't get any voting rights or anything like that. We would just call on you if we need your particular talents."

"I don't know about that, I technically have two jobs. I run security for Tony Marcus and the government keeps me on-call as a specialist. No, I'm not telling you what I specialize in, don't ask for that information. It could get your whole family dead."

"Is Mr. Marcus going to call you out for jobs?"

"No, I'm going to tell you something that can't leave this room. I'm not even sure if I have told Fiona yet. I have an identical twin brother. When I told Tony I was staying here, he called my brother in. My rep as his bodyguard is spotless, so as long as people believe it's me by his side nobody is going to mess with him. Might make a couple trips a year to keep up with him, but I would ask Fi to go with me on those."

"How are you going to support my sister? I can't Imagine Mr. Marcus paying you not to work, government jobs pay shit."

"I have enough money in the bank for ten lifetimes. Never had anyone to spend it on before."

"Well think about the consultant gig, I've gotta go. The girls have been down at Bella's for a while now. Miranda seems to forget she is pregnant. Sometimes I catch her doing the strangest things. Last night I caught her at the club house scrubbing tables down with disinfectant."

"That's not strange."

"It is when it isn't her job, I can't keep her still. I practically have to hold her down to get her to go to sleep at night."

"You aren't doing something right if you can't keep your woman in bed."

"Bro, just wait until it's your turn. She keeps jumping on my cock the way she does, she's gonna break it clean off. I'm not telling you to knock up my sister or anything but damn, pregnant women are horny and demanding."

I am still laughing when he leaves.

Chapter 8
Fiona

I decided to walk to Bella's; it's only a couple blocks away. Knowing my brother and his club, they'll have the few roads around the coffee shop blocked off. Nobody in this town would dare piss off a member of Wolfsbane Ridge. So I feel safe. Besides, I have my gun locked and loaded.

The first person I see is Butcher, the Road Captain for the MC. He is sitting on a bench at the bus stop. He isn't even trying to blend in; I can't help but laugh at him. Even in grade school he stood out. Then I see Bear across the street. There seems to be either a club member or a prospect on every corner of every intersection.

When I walk in the door, I am greeted by Miranda, Bella and Mina. They are sitting at the table already.

"Is Hayden coming?" I ask

"No, she wants to spend some time with her daughter."

I look at the three women sitting at the table with me. To think that just a few months ago I didn't know them. Pulling the frog prank created a bond between us. I can still hear that guy screaming, when I close my eyes. It was the most fun I've had since leaving White Summer five years ago.

"Please invite Lily next time." Bella begs me. She has been kicking my ass in self defense classes. I like her.

"I don't know about that, Bells, she isn't known by the club. The guys might flip out if we invite outsiders. She is one of my best friends, but I don't want her affected by the shit we deal with."

After that the conversation quickly turned to baby talk. Mina had her baby shower a few weeks ago, now she wants to plan one for Miranda. The ideas for games are getting pretty wild.

Bella suggested a Lego walk. She said we would fill a room with Lego's and make the guys walk across them. Whichever one made it across would get a 'Daddy award'. We all picture our guys getting taken out by Lego's.

Mina wanted the dirty diaper game. You melt different candy bars into a diaper. The contestant has to lick the 'poop' and guess what candy bar it is. Miranda wants a baby food taste test.

We are all laughing hysterically, when Mina grabs her side.

"Umm ladies, I gotta pee." As she stands up to leave the table, her pants get soaked.

"No, you already did." I point out. Everyone but Bella starts laughing again.

"No, her water broke." You could have heard a pin drop When Bella said that.

The silence was broken by Mina, "Well I was thinking about pouring a glass of water on the floor to prank you all, but I decided not to. I didn't want to leave a mess for Sunshine."

Just then Blood walked in. something in our faces must have alerted him there was an issue because he immediately went on guard.

"What's going on? I expected to walk into a hen party, not a funeral." He asks looking to Mina as if she is our spokesperson

"I'm having a baby."

"Yes, I know Mina; you need to get some sleep."

"No, Blood. I am having a baby now."

I watch as the blood drains from his face. I start laughing; now everyone is looking at me.

Pointing at my brother, "Look how pale he is. The blood is draining from his face. Get it? Blood is losing blood." Miranda and Bella snicker but nobody finds it as funny as I do. If looks could kill my brother would be committing murder right now.

"Mina, what time is Timber supposed to be picking you up?"

"In about fifteen minutes."

"Call him. If he hasn't left yet he can grab your go bag. Bella are you her birth coach?"

"Yes"

"Good. Call the hospital; let them know she is on her way. Then call Blade. I assume he is watching the kids."

"No, we had already planned for them to stay at Mom's tonight. She offered to give us some time alone."

He is giving out orders. I wonder what he is going to tell me to do.

"Miranda dear, we will follow them to the hospital. We aren't staying. We are going to help Mina settle in, and then you are going to bed. You haven't slept much at all this week"

She looks like she wants to argue with him but one look at Mina stops her.

"Fiona," he pauses to think. "Fiona, go home. I'll have Butcher walk you back. Before you get all hot, think about it. The hospital staff won't see you as family and it could be hours before the baby is actually born."

Sadly I have to admit, my brother is right, so while he goes outside and yells down the street for Butcher, we say our goodbyes. Mina hugs me, promising to have someone update me every couple of hours.

I can't resist poking at Blood when he comes back in. "You know you could have just texted him."

"Shut up Brat." He growls at me. I'm speechless. My brother, the boy I stitched up almost daily when we were kids. The man that covered up a double homicide for me, just growled at me. My jaw drops. I can't believe my brother just growled at me.

"Close your mouth Fiona; you'll catch flies if you keep your jaw hanging open like that. You know I love you but now is not the time for your humor."

Just then Butcher charges through the door, gun drawn looking for trouble.

"Butcher, walk my sister home."

"You screamed down the street like a Banshee, for me to walk your sister home? Why didn't you just text me?"

I lose it, I'm doubled over laughing. When Mina pipes in, "That's what she said." I hit the floor. I can't even stand up, I'm laughing so hard. I crawl over to Miranda and rub her belly.

"I can't wait for you to be born Little Bean. You and Me, we are going to drive your Daddy crazy."

Butcher just looks at all of us like we have lost our minds. "What is going on, Blood?"

"Mina is in labor. Timber and Blade are on their way here. I'm following them to the hospital. Please make sure my sister gets home safe. Thank you."

Everyone clears out pretty quickly after that. I take a minute to calm myself, before telling Butcher I'm ready. Bella left the keys with him, so he can lock up   behind   us.

Baratta

Fiona is in a strange mood when she gets back. She marches into the apartment and plops herself down in my lap. Throwing her arms around my neck she kisses me.

"I love you."

"Fi, are you drunk? I thought you weren't drinking tonight?"

"Nope not drunk. Just happy."

"Why are you happy?"

"Mina is having a baby."

"Yes I know but why is this making you happy?"

"No I mean Mina is having a baby now, tonight. She is on her way to the hospital."

"I still don't get why you are being weird."

"Adrenaline rush, from watching my brother act a fool."

"Explain"

"Well first he turned white as a ghost, and then he started giving orders like a drill sergeant. To top it off instead of texting Butcher, he went outside Bella's Brew and screamed down the street for him. I asked why he didn't just text. Butcher thought World War three was starting and charged in with his gun drawn. Then when he asked why Blood didn't just text. Mina said, and I quote, that's what she said."

She snuggles into my arms, "Do you want a baby? I mean not now but eventually. Have you ever thought about having kids?"

"Before you, I never met a woman that I would want to have kids with."

"And now?"

"I'll give you anything you want."

"Well, I don't want one now but someday. We could practice until we are ready."

"Practice what?"

"Making a baby."

You don't have to tell me twice, I swing her up in my arms and carry her to the bedroom.

Chapter 9
Baratta

I thought I did a good job wearing Fiona out, but I was wrong. She walked the floor all night long; jumping every time she received a text. Finally around 6 a.m. she got the news, Hawk Creed was born. She fell into bed exhausted.

I took care of Bleu this morning and let her sleep. But it's almost time for the shop to open. I still have a pounding headache but my body is mostly healed, so I decided to wake her up with food.

"Wakey Wakey, eggs and bakey"

"Hmmmm, what?"

"Food babe, wake up and eat, it's almost time for work."

"You cook?" she looks at me with surprise in her eyes. That's when I realize I haven't cooked for her.

"I'll have you know I'm a damn good cook."

"I'm keeping you forever."

"I thought we established that already. You said you love me. Nothing you can do would get rid of me now."

"You love me too, you cooked for me." She says as she takes the plate from me.

"Are you sure about that?"

"Yep, I know you aren't 100 percent yet. Here you are taking care of me."

"You are right, I love you."

Fiona starts choking on the bite of eggs she just took. I pat her on the back, trying to help her clear it.

"You said you love me."

"Yes and …"

"It's just I know you feel it, but I never expected to hear you say it, at least not for a while longer."

"If you didn't have to go to work, I would climb in that bed and show you how much I love you."

"If I didn't have to go to work, I would let you."

She finishes eating, and then heads for the shower. As soon as she is up I climb into bed. My head hits the pillow and I groan, from the pounding that won't let up.

"I heard that." Fi says stepping back out of the bathroom. "Maybe I should take you to the hospital?"

"No, not happening. You are not using me as an excuse to go see the baby."

"Awe, Party pooper." she fake pouts. "But seriously, maybe someone should check out your head."

"Everything else has healed up; I just can't seem to shake this headache. I've had worse; I promise I'll be fine."

"Maybe you need something stronger than over the counter crap?" She thinks for a minute then throws open her closet door and goes digging through boxes.

"Fi what are you doing?"

"Last year I sprained my ankle, the Doc gave me some prescription strength stuff. I think I still have it in here. I hate taking pills. Eureka!"

She hands me the bottle to read while she gets me a glass of water. It's a low dose pain killer I've taken before. I know it won't do much but if it takes the edge off the headache and lets me sleep, it's worth it.

I'm very close to sleep when I feel Fi's lips on my forehead. "Sleep well."

Fiona

It doesn't feel right, leaving Baratta like this. I'm more concerned about his headache than I let on. I have to keep reminding myself, I'm only going to be downstairs.

The shop has been open for about an hour when a customer comes in with a yappy little Chihuahua. The yapping wouldn't bother me but the little fucker keeps jumping up on the client while I'm trying to work!

"Lily! Arin!" I call out for whichever one isn't busy at the moment.

It's Lily that answers me first. Tossing her my keys, I ask her to go get Bleu's crate from my apartment. "Be very quiet, please. Bar is sleeping."

"You can't put my little Mousie in a crate!" The customer acts like I'm threatening to choke her dog, which I might just do next.

"Either the little fucker goes in a crate or you leave here with one-third of a tattoo. AND you will pay full price for it. You're lucky I have a dog crate or you would be outta here right now." She gives in and Mouse is put in the crate.

I'm finished with her and waiting on my next client to arrive, when I realize Lily never gave me back my keys.

"Hey Lily" her head pops up from where she is doing some touch ups.

"Where'd you put my keys?"

"I left them on the counter; you were busy with that little bitch. I don't mean the dog either."

"Remind me to put her in the black book. I refuse to do any more work for her."

"Gotcha boss"

I start looking for my keys but my next client comes in distracting me with work, the missing keys slipping right out of my mind.

Just when I finish up my third tattoo of the night, a loud banging sound hits the ceiling above us. We all stop what we're doing and look up. There are more bangs and thumps, it sounds like an elephant is charging through my apartment, followed by a few moments of silence, before my brain kicks in.

"Baratta!" I yell as I run for the back door. As soon as it slams open I see a red truck fishtailing its way out of the back parking lot. I quickly take note of the make and model before running back upstairs.

My door is wide open with my keychain dangling from the lock. Pulling my gun while I enter, I can hear Bleu whining but I don't go to him. Slowly walking through each room, it looks like a tornado hit inside, art torn off the walls, furniture flipped over and my stalker pictures tossed everywhere.

My bed, where I left Baratta sleeping, is empty. Bleu is locked in my closet. Weirdly. My bathroom looks untouched. That's where I'm standing when Lily takes my hand, leading me back down to the shop.

"Everyone out!" She calls before we are even inside the door.

"But my Tattoo isn't complete." One Customer whines.

"Make an appointment to come back."

"I don't want to come back."

There is no time for this bullshit; I grab the guy by his collar. "You will leave, you will call for an appointment and we won't charge you anything for the work. If you don't like it, I will call my brother. You know who he is; now get out of my shop!"

Mad Dog/Clint/ Harold

I was standing outside my girlfriend's tattoo parlor when she opened. Nobody sees me, I'm invisible. Ghost has been hiding in her apartment up stairs. I wonder if she knows he's there.

I bet he's hiding there to try and catch me. "Run, Run as fast you can. You can't catch the gingerbread man or the Mad Dog." I laugh to myself.

I've been sending her pictures, hoping and praying she sees them. I want her to know I'm watching. I'll save her from him. That yappy dog is annoying her. Maybe I'll follow that chick home and take care of it for her.

Knowing my girl won't go anywhere until the shop closes, I start to walk away when I see Lily drop my Fiona's keys on the counter.

My heart starts beating rapidly; I can feel it pounding out of my chest. I know now is my chance. No one even notices me walking in the front door, then out again. I look down at the keys in my hand, saying a prayer of thanks.

I run down the street to get my truck, knowing that getting into the apartment will be the easy part but I need my truck to get him away from my love.

Pulling into the parking lot behind her building, I grab my bag from under the seat. It should have everything I need.

No longer hiding my presence I walk up the steps. The door opens right up, thanks to the keys. I have my gun out in case Ghost gets the drop on me but the only sound I hear is my girl's puppy. Making my way room by room, I finally find him, he's sleeping in her bed!

"Bastard! Thought you could steal my girl!" I yell but he doesn't move.

"What is wrong with you?" I question, and then I see the pill bottle on the night table and start laughing. I can't believe it, my girl is crafty. She drugged the bastard for me.

After putting on my gloves, I get a sedative from my bag. I don't know how many pills he took. I need to make sure he stays asleep until I get him to my little hide away.

Giving the injection time to do its magic, I go on a cleaning frenzy. I don't want anything left of Ghost in my girl's home after I take him out. Tearing pictures from the walls, trashing furniture in case he sat on it, I even smash the dishes. I won't let my girl eat off anything he has touched.

I find the pictures I've been sending my girl hidden in the back of a kitchen cabinet.

"I knew it! I knew you were hiding these, bad Ghosty." I spread them around so my girl knows I'm the man that saved her.

I almost tossed her bathroom, too. But my girl needs her makeup to be beautiful. So I back off. The puppy has been hiding under the bed this whole time. I saw how much my girl loves him when she takes him out for walks. So I put him in the closet where he won't get hurt.

Ghost is bigger than me, but we have the same training. I can lift a man twice my size. Flipping him over my shoulder, I head for the door. Oops, I dropped him. I 'accidentally' drop him a couple more times.   This   is   fun!

Chapter 10
Fiona

Lily grabbed my cell phone and called my brother. He's here now with a couple of club members. They think I am in shock but I'm not. I am planning. The club has resources I don't, so I'm going to let them do the leg work.

After going upstairs, Blood and Timber have a conversation with Lily. I let Blood lead me out to his bike.

"Come on sis, I'm taking you to the clubhouse." I don't respond but I climb on the back of his bike. He places a helmet on my head before taking off.

When he gets to the clubhouse, he puts his keys in his pocket. However; when he turns to watch the other bikes pull in, I slip them out. He has no clue, even though he taught me that trick.

Leading me through the clubhouse, Blood takes me down a hall that I know has offices but he opens a door I have never been through before. This part of the clubhouse is completely off limits to anyone not a member.

To my surprise, Snake is sitting in front of a bank of computers.

"Fiona, tell Snake what the truck looked like."

"It was a red Ford F150; it had a black bed liner. The back window was cracked. The plates were from out of state but I didn't see them long enough to make out what state."

Timber puts a chair behind me and tells me to sit. I only listen because I know it's not time to fight yet. Someone else brings me food, but I can't eat. I'm too busy watching the video screens in front of Snake. I notice something odd on one of the screens.

"Is that? Is that my apartment? Blood, why does the club have a camera in my apartment?"

"The club doesn't have a camera in your place. Baratta has a camera in your place. He gave me the code for emergency use only."

I'm not sure how much time passes, although it feels like forever. Snake is busy typing away doing his thing, when he suddenly shouts, "Got him Boss." They all crowd around him, as he walks them through the night. Nobody notices me.

"See here on this screen, he is watching the shop. That's from the camera in the bakery across the street. Then we switch over to the hardware store cam, he must have left his truck there. From there we can follow him camera to camera until he gets out of town. Last sighting is at the stop light on the North side.

"Isn't that out by Brown road, towards the airport?" Timber looks to Blood.

"Yeah, Brown is where I picked up his bike."

Going by what Baratta told me about the accident I have a pretty good idea where they are. It surprises me that Blood hasn't picked up on it yet but I'll not be volunteering the information.

"Church!" Timber calls out, gathering up the men. I start to follow, knowing they won't let me in. "FiFi." My head snaps up. Blood knows to never ever call me that.

"Sorry, just wanted to make sure you hear me. I know what you're thinking. It's not possible, I burned it down. You can't come to church either. You already know it's not allowed. Go see the baby, Mina came home this afternoon."

I lurk around the hall watching as the men file into the room. Blood kisses me on the forehead then shuts the door in my face.

This is my chance. Scoping out the clubhouse to be sure of where the prospects are doesn't take me long and before anyone notices, I'm riding out on my brother's bike.

I only look back once I'm through the gate. I see the guys running out the door. It's too late to stop me. I know something about the old home place that Blood doesn't. He moved out when he turned 18, leaving me behind with the Monster.

He wasn't there when the cabin was built. I wouldn't have known it was there if I hadn't been nosey and followed the Monster into the woods one night. One peek in the window was all it took for me to run home and hide in my closet.

Blood

"Do we follow, boss?" One of the Prospects asks me. I don't even know which one.

"Not yet. I taught her to ride, she'll be safe. I know where she's going but last I checked there was nothing left out there."

Timber puts his hand on my shoulder, "I can have one of the guys follow her and keep us updated. You know she can handle herself."

"But she shouldn't have to, Timber. I never should have left her in that house."

"Blood, your sister isn't a little girl anymore. Besides, she handled herself pretty good back then."

"It should have been me that took those two fuckers to their grave. If only she had told me. I'd have made them suffer." I growl at the memory.

"You were there to put them in the hole though. Several of us were. She has the same fire inside that we all see within you. That's why she didn't tell any of us. It's why she just rode away on her own. And I'm willing to bet she knows something we don't."

"Anyone got a quiet ride? Someone that can have eyes on her but stay out of sight?"

"We got this." He grabs one of the prospects, sending him out to watch over my sister. "Stay in contact."

Baratta

I wake up with a groan. I thought the pain meds would help my headache but if anything it is worse than before. My whole body aches. It feels like I went a couple rounds in the gym. It isn't until I reach up to grab my head that I realize I can't.

I'm duct taped to a chair, in the middle of what appears to be a one room cabin. This can't be a club cabin; they are much nicer than this. Plus Blood checked out all the tenants. I don't even have to see his face to know who has me.

"Amico, what are you doing?"

"No, tu no non sono mio amico"

"English, Amico mio."

"You speak Italian then tell me to use English. Always the double standard with you. Nothing changes."

"What are you talking about? You were my best friend."

"I was never your friend! You take from people, always taking! You take my job, you take my family, and now you try to take my girl. Tony Marcus, he is always choosing you over me. I was better bag man than you but did he ever tell me, I do good job? No, always praise for the little Ghost.

My Papa steals a little bit of coke, does Tony Marcus have compassion? No, he sends the Little Ghost. Only Little Ghost he doesn't kill me like Tony says, he says to me. Go to Italy, train for army, be good for you. I think Little Ghost good friend. Then Little Ghost follows him to army. Mad Dog doing good, getting awards, bosses like Mad Dog. Little Ghost can't stand it, has to be better than Mad Dog at everything."

I don't interrupt his rant or correct him. I can tell he isn't in his right mind anymore. We were trained to blend in but his speech is reverting back to the way it was before I saved his life. His broken English is a throwback to the immigrant boy, with a deadbeat dad.

"Mad Dog tired of being second best. Ghost can hide but Mad Dog rip apart his enemies. Do you know what happened to Mad Dog when he tries to leave army? They hunt me! Me! They say, no! Army or dead. I pick army."

I think I see a shadow outside the only window in the cabin. I have to keep Mad Dog talking and distracted. I'm not sure who it is but I hope someone is here to help me.

"Mad Dog, Amico. Tell me about your girl. Why do you think I stole your girl?"

He slaps me, "I am not you friend! Stop saying that! My girl, she is beautiful work of art. People they say tattoo not art, but my girl she draw everything freehand. All her work original, she turn ugly people into beautiful people. No more talk. I kill you then go kill yappy dog. Fiona she love garbage puppy, but want to kick yappy dog. I take care of for her."

"Amico, why did you send all those pictures to Fiona?"

"I am not you friend! I show my girl, I watch out for her. I keep her safe."

"Why does she call you Clint?"

"Clint safe, American name. My mom she must be on drugs when she name me. Who gives name Harold to Italian man? The people they call me Harry. I not Harry. I Mad Dog, but for her I be Clint. No more talk, yappy dog waiting for me."

I watch him raise his gun and take aim but before he can pull the trigger the door is thrown open and my worst nightmare burst into the cabin.

A tremor of fear snakes through my body, as he spins with the gun ready to fire.

"NO!" I scream, I can't tell from where I am who pulled the trigger but the blast of the 9mm echoes off the walls. When Mad Dog falls to the floor with a bullet hole right between his eyes, I almost can't believe it's over.

"Did you miss me?" Fiona asks as she holsters her gun. She doesn't wait for an answer. Fi straddles my lap and kisses me until we are both out of breath.

"I have one question for you."

"Hmm?"

"Who or what is yappy dog?"

"I'll tell you while I cut off this tape." She proceeds to tell me about her night. By the end of the yappy dog story, I'm not restrained anymore. So I pull her into my lap. We probably would have stayed like that for hours, if three hot headed MC members didn't charge through the door ten minutes later.

Fiona spins around so she is facing them. "Your timing leaves a little something to be desired."

Timber, Blade and Blood are just standing there looking at her. The silence is almost creepier than listening to Mad Dog's rant. It's finally broken by Blood.

"Fiona, how long has this cabin been here and why didn't you tell me about it back at the clubhouse."

She ignores him when I turn her head back to me, "Where are we Babe?"

She tries to look at Blood but I don't let her turn away.

"Fine" she crosses her arms over her chest. "Timber, are the woods clear?" I don't understand why she is asking him that, until I hear his answer. "Nobody can hear you but us."

"We grew up here, on this land. Me and Blood. That's probably why Mad Dog chose this place. It's still in my name but I never come here. Our Dad was awesome, I remember him swinging me around in his arms, playing ball with Blood. Until one day he disappeared, just poof gone like he never existed. The same day he went missing was the day Step-Monster showed up. He wore Dad's clothes. He rode Dad's bike; it was almost like he was trying to be Dad. I was five or six?" She looks to Blood for confirmation.

"Six, I was nine."

"The first year wasn't so bad, but when Blood turned ten the monster decided he was old enough to learn to fight. Not kicking, punching, and boxing kind of fighting. No, that was too clean for him. He wanted Blood to fight him with a knife.

I was seven the first time I thought my brother was going to bleed to death. By the time I was ten I could sew stitches better than any doctor in this town. When Blood turned eighteen he ran like hell to get out of here. I didn't have my brother to protect me anymore.

He started out with just slapping me around. He said I wouldn't learn to fight like my brother because I was just a useless little girl. I did learn to hide though. I spent my high school years hiding from him.

When I was seventeen, I saw him acting weird. So I followed him into the woods. He came to this cabin.

When I peek through the window I could see he had a woman tied up and he was hurting her. I ran home to hide in my closet for the rest of the night.

I must have made a noise or something that let him know that I was there. He got more violent as the days went by. Instead of just hitting me and cussing at me, he started grabbing me. Mom would just watch as he fondled me. He would make comments like; you are a big girl now.

I ran to the clubhouse and begged Blood to teach me how to shoot. He's the one that gave me my first gun. I was shooting better than him pretty fast. He called it beginner's luck, I called it determination. I slept with the gun under my pillow every night after that.

"Do I have to tell the rest?" She looks at me but asks the room.

Timber gently says, "I have just one more question, please. Blood has been begging you to sell this place for years. We buried those assholes on the mountain, miles away from here. Why won't you let it go?"

"I know the house is gone. I'm glad Blood burned it to the ground. But, what if Dad comes back?"

No one in the room has the heart to tell her, he is probably dead. So I put a stop to the conversation.

"No more questions, you don't have to say another word."

"Good can we go home now?"

I pick her up and walk out of the cabin.

Chapter 11
Fiona

"Holy shit this place is huge! I've been lost for the past hour. It's like a maze or something." I say as I walk across the beautiful rose garden.

"You'll learn your way around the more you visit. This place has been in our family for several generations. I personally love it here."

Something in the sound of Baratta's voice sounds off so I fully turn to look at him. That's when I notice that while this man looks nearly identical to my man, it can't possibly be him.

"I thought you were Bar." I study him some more seeing the tiny differences.

"Alessandro mentioned that you call him by a nickname. Most people do not realize there are two of us. My name is Giovanni Baratta but my friends call me Gio." He smiles the same crooked smile that Baratta gets when being mischievous.

"I see you've met my brother." Baratta comments as he walks up from behind.

"I thought he was you until I really looked at him." Baratta walks up, putting his arm around me.

"I told her that most do not realize the slight differences."

"It's good that she did, I wouldn't want to kill my brother for her making the mistake and kissing the wrong lips." Bar says as his brother laughs.

"Why do I get violence? It would have been her mistake." Gio laughingly picks at his brother.

"Because I know you. You would have gone along with it as if you were really me. You've done so before."

"Ah, but I knew those few were not for you. The one meant for you could never mistake me for you. Plus, you never tried to kill me for it." Giovanni says in all seriousness.

"I think he has a point." I smile at the two of them.

"So how long are the two of you staying?" Gio asks Bar. The two of them walk towards the huge lake and I slowly follow, giving them space to talk amongst themselves.

Baratta

Spending time with my brother is something I've not done since we were younger. We both went into the military; only I went a little farther within the government agency that trained me to be a killer.

Gio was the opposite of me when we were growing up. He was always more popular and out-going through school, while I was more with-drawn and antisocial.

Everyone knew that I was quite different. I didn't cry either. Not even when our dog died. I watched from the sidelines wondering why my brother was screaming as the dog lay there bleeding out from the old bear trap that it had gotten caught in. I remember thinking that the blood was very pretty, almost like paint.

"She seems to be your match in every way." Giovanni breaks the silence while we walk.

"What do you mean?" I'm curious as to how he sees the two of us.

He looks off across the distance like he is trying to find the right words.

"You always had this...tiny spark in your eyes. It was like you saw the world differently than I ever did. Than most people ever did. You were colder. Never allowing others to touch you for instance. Not even hugs. But you touch her like you have done so your entire life. Easily. You don't tense up when she touches you back."

"That's how I knew she was different the night I met her. It was easy for me when I was with her that night. Then the next morning when I returned to the hotel room to find her gone it pissed me off. I felt like I couldn't breathe." I look to my brother as I explain. While we were both very different, he was always there for me to talk to.

"And now you feel free, no?" He smiles.

"Yes. She means everything to me now. We even have a dog." Gio laughs at the dog comment.

We both look behind us to see Fi picking flowers close to the water's edge. She smiles in our direction when she notices the two of us watching.

"When do you think you'll ask her to marry you and give me a niece or nephew?"

"As soon as we get back, I need to ask her brother's permission first."

"I've heard a lot about Blood from Uncle Tony. I've also heard about what he did to Ray before they fed his corpse to the alligators. You think you can handle a brother in law as ruthless as yourself?" Gio raises his eyebrows at me.

"I just have to make sure I keep my skills up so that he can't catch me. I like my manhood exactly where it's located." I give a mock shudder causing Giovanni to double over in laughter.

"What's so funny?" Fiona asks when she walks up to where we are.

"The things men should not be made to eat." I explain with a serious face and my brother falls to the ground laughing so hard he starts to turn red.

"He looks like he's not getting enough air." Fiona just stands there watching Gio on the ground with a straight face as well.

"Well I'm not giving him mouth to mouth." I murmur still watching my brother.

"Me either, there's no telling where his mouth has been plus I only just met him." My girl smiles in my direction before once again looking down.

My brother finally stops laughing so hard as he looks up at the two of us standing there.

"You two are perfect for each other. You'd both just stand there and watch me die." He stands up, shaking his head.

"We still love you though." I say to his retreating back.

"Oh, I can tell that!" He throws over his shoulder.

I look down at Fi as she looks up. Within seconds, she's giggling.

"I love you."

"I love you too, Bar. I wouldn't have let him die though if he was really hurt."

"Neither would I but we don't have to let him know that. Come on, Dinner should be ready."

We walk back to the house in the direction that Giovanni went. I'm uncertain as to what has been going on with him. He seems a little quieter these days but if he wanted me to know, he would tell me. Hopefully he will visit us in Montana as often as he can. I really would like to be closer to my own twin.

I can only hope that whatever is bothering him isn't something that will get him hurt. I'd hate to have to get in the middle. But I will kill to keep my family safe.

"We both would." Fiona whispers. I hadn't realized I had said that out loud.

I hug her closer to me. Her comment making me feel happier than I can ever recall being.

"I know and that is why we are perfect together."

"It's good that you realize that. I'd hate it if I had to kill you for trying to leave me." She smiles wickedly.

"I'd hate that too." We both laugh as we walk the rest of the way to the house.

I never thought life could ever be so perfect.

***

Hope you enjoyed Baratta's Darkness.

Continue on the next pages for sneak peaks of upcoming titles including
Poison Pen Book 2, Lily's Shadow.

Poison Pen Book 2
Lily's Shadow
Lilyanna

It has been almost six months since I moved to White Summer. My best friend Fiona opened her tattoo shop in town and hired me as her office manager-artist. One of her requirements for me to work for her has been to attend self defense classes.

I was doing really well in my class in Seattle, even taking extra classes because I love it so much. Fiona has promised to teach me kickboxing; she is really good at it. Sometimes she even wins against her own trainer, Austin.

After Fiona's boyfriend was kidnapped by a stalker recently, I asked her to increase my training. I even want to learn how to use a gun. It was my fault. I'm the one that left her keys on the counter.

No matter how many times she tells me it wasn't. I can't help but feel guilty about it. I don't ever want to see one of my friend's look so helpless again. Good thing Fiona is a kick ass bitch and took down the monster all on her own.

Fiona and Baratta are leaving for vacation to Italy after Miranda has her baby, so I need to up my game. I will be running the tattoo shop on my own for the first time. She's depending on me to keep everything running smoothly while they are gone.

I have my first martial arts class with Austin today. I'm really excited about it but I'm nervous as hell too. Austin is an attractive man. Every time I look at him my heart starts racing. I doubt he even realizes I exist beyond being a client of Hay's Den.

I'm about to grab my gym bag to head out of the door when Loki, my German shepherd starts to whine. Looking over at him, I see that he has his food bowl hanging from his mouth.

"I'm sorry; did I forget to fill it this morning?" I laugh as he hops around excitedly as I take the bowl from him.

Filling the bowl, I place it on the floor. He licks my face as I stroke his fur.

"My sweet boy." I murmur into his head.

I got him several years ago from a trainer I met while at the inker's expo. He trained guard dogs for the elite and gave me a hell of a deal for him. He's been my constant companion ever since. One thing is for sure, he'd eat someone's face off if I told him to. That comes in handy for a single woman these days.

Smiling at the thought, I pick up my gym bag and walk out the door.

Austin

Moving to White Summer a little over a year ago has been the best decision I have ever made. I am working at Hay's den, my boss is my best friend and life is more laid back here. Something I've needed for quite some time.

I'm no longer fighting professionally although I miss it sometimes. The roar of the fans, the adrenaline rush of winning, the women throwing their bras and panties in the ring after a match.

I don't miss the circus created by my ex wife though. I found out she was sleeping with one of my sponsors and kicked her out. In retaliation she accused me of domestic violence.

After that I hired a private investigator. I discovered more than I ever expected. For example the reason the paparazzi always seemed to know where we were is because she called them.

About 2 months after the separation, I found out she was pregnant too. When confronted she said the baby wasn't mine. At that point I just wanted her out of my life so I didn't fight anything she wanted in the divorce.

After that, it didn't take Hayden long to convince me to move here with her. She was going through her own shit around that time as well. I probably would have killed her ex-husband if the police hadn't found him first.

My ex has started up her shit again lately. I had messages on my phone from her again last night. I didn't even bother checking them. Wish the bitch would get a fucking clue. I'm no longer interested.

I'm in the gym pounding the shit out of a bag when Lily comes in for her first advanced class with me. She has been in the beginner's class with Hayden, but after some shit down at the tattoo parlor she works in she really kicked it up a notch and we feel she's ready.

We just finished class, I tell her to head to the shower when a commotion breaks out at the front desk. I can hear Hayden yelling all the way back here so I know it's not good.

Lily and I approach cautiously. We can see a crowd gathered behind the desk. Hayden is facing us, yelling at a woman that has her back to us. The woman seems familiar but I can't see her face yet.

"Get out of my building!" Hayden yells.

"I am not leaving until I see him." The woman yells back. I know that voice; it's one I never wanted to hear again.

"If you don't leave on your own, I will have you escorted out!"

"Fine you tell him if he ever wants to see his kid, I'm staying out at the Wolfsbane ridge cabins."

"Not for long." I hear one of the guys in the crowd murmur, just before she turns around and sees me.

"What do you want Erica?"

Instead of the defiant woman arguing with HayHay, she suddenly turns into a simpering damsel.

"I want you to come home, our daughter needs you."

"You said the baby wasn't mine, and this is my home."

"I lied, please give us another chance."

If I am sure of one thing, it is that I don't want her back. She ruined my career, my reputation and my life. I feel the eyes of everyone looking at me, so I do the first thing I can think of.

Throwing my arm around Lily, "Erica, meet my fiancée Lily." I'm hoping like hell Lily will go along with it.

I can feel her stiffen up before she relaxes into me. Looking down, Lily smiles up at me before turning her eyes to Erica.

"What about our daughter?" Erica whines.

"I'll contact our attorney first thing in the morning about getting a DNA test. But be forewarned Erica, if that baby belongs to Austin? We plan to go after sole custody. And we *will* win. My father happens to be Governor Mark Harris from California." Lily smirks at Erica's wide eyed expression. "Now get the fuck out!"

I hear the commotion of some of the Wolfsbane Ridge guys escort Erica out but I can't seem to take my eyes off of Lily. I'm shocked speechless at her admission to being the daughter of one of the most well known Governors. I'm also shocked at my body's reaction to having her in my arms. I've tried very hard to keep it professional where she is concerned. If she remains in my arms though, all bets are off.

Coming Soon..

Night Howler's MC New Orleans
Book 1
Buzz

Prologue

Buzz

Several years ago, my little sister was raped and murdered. Her killer was never caught. She had been emailing a guy she had met in an online chat room. Even though the authorities had his name he used online, every lead came to a dead end. It didn't stop me from continuing the search.

A few weeks ago I caught a break. Another programmer I knew from when I was still in the service stumbled across the same name with a different unique IP address that constantly bounces around making it almost impossible to follow.

However, follow it I did and where it winds up leading me has me second guessing what I am planning.

I'll take something of his. His beautiful sister Markayla. But we don't hurt innocents. I will protect her as best I can. I plan on her step brother paying for what he did to my sister with his own blood. What I don't plan for is falling hard for my enemy's sister.

Even after all of these years I can't believe my mother was stupid enough to fall for my step father. I have never doubted he had something to do with her disappearance. I've just never been able to prove it.

You would think that with her gone, I'd be free of the Marcus family. Unfortunately for me, my step father adopted me when he married my mother.

My step brother absolutely hates me and I am certain that our Papa is the only one keeping him from doing whatever he wanted to me.

The look I see in his eyes any time I run into him while I am out with friends or a date scares me to my core. I refuse to let him know just how scared of him I really am.

If anything ever happens to Papa or I become expendable in his eyes, I will need to run and run fast. Getting away before he gives me to Joe to do whatever he wants with me, will take a miracle.

Coming November 2021
https://books2read.com/BuzzNewOrleans

Wolfsbane Ridge MC, Book 1
Timber's Fairy

CHAPTER 1
Mina

It was such a beautiful day today and I was glad I had decided to take a break from my computer to go have coffee with my best friend. Winter had been brutal this year with all the snow and ice. I didn't really mind the weather too much. It was one of the things that drew me to this area a year ago. Seeing the snow covered mountains off in the distance no matter what time of year, took my breath away.

"Morning, Bella!" I called out as I walked into the local coffee shop.

"Hey, Mina, I'm glad you are finally here. I can use a break! Find a seat. I'll get your usual and join you for a few minutes." Bella was one of the first few people to welcome me into their little community. She owned and operated *"Bella's Brew"*. Although we had only met 1 year ago, most people not from here mistook us for sisters. We were both slender, stood 5'4", straight black onyx hair with blue eyes and 25 years old. Some of the local townsfolk called us the Pixie sisters.

"So what's on your schedule today?" she said as she set our coffee down.

"I have a skype meeting with my editor later this afternoon but other than that there's just a long boring day of retyping corrections. Why? Did you finally decide you are ready to go get drinks with me later?"

"Yeah, I have. My Mom is driving me insane since she moved in with me. I will be SO glad when she can finally find her own place."

"So that's what it takes to get my BFF to go out with me. Move her 3 times divorced mother in with her."

"You are such a bitch some times." She said as we both laughed.

"Bella, I know it's hard but she's your mother. Surely she's not being that bad"

"Mina, I swear to God you have no idea! She did my laundry the other day although I have asked numerous times that she NOT go into my room. She did it anyway. Then when I got home she proceeded to inform me that it was really no wonder I was still a 25 year old single woman since I was still wearing what she referred to as granny panties!!"

"Bahahahaha! I am so sorry Bella but that shit is hilarious! Your mom is a total trip. I think she's fun to be around."

"Yeah, well, you are not the one that has to live with her. The breakfast crowd will be rolling in soon. You want to meet me here at around 7:00 and we'll go have drinks?"

Bella had no idea how much I envied her having her mom around. My parents had passed away 10 years ago leaving my oldest brother to raise a teenage girl. I checked my watch as I gathered my things to walk towards the door. "Sure, I'll see ya at 7. Hope the town is ready for the Pixie Sisters again!" Both of us were laughing as we remembered our last drunken night out.

******

I was late! Bella had already been texting my phone like crazy. I pulled up at *Bella's Brew* at 7:40. Bella of course was waiting for me at the front entrance and tried to climb into the front seat before I even come to a complete stop. I couldn't stop the giggle as I watched her struggle into my truck.

"I don't understand why in the world you have to have such a tall ass truck. Is it a *"Southern Thang"* as you like to say all the time? Or are you compensating for something?" She said with a smirk on her face.

"Ha-ha. Just shut up and get your seatbelt on so we can get on the road."

"Whatever! It's not like we aren't already late anyway. Bet you were so into your writing, you never looked at the clocked. They make alarm clocks for a reason ya know." She made it sound like she was put out by my lateness but the smile on her face told a different story.

"I know they do and that is precisely why I refuse to have one. I don't like distractions while I am working. And you know this already which is why I know you didn't actually start getting ready until 7:00."

"Yeah yeah, so where do we want to go tonight?"

"I thought maybe we would go over to *Blackcat Bar & Grill*. We can eat before we get good and started on those shots we love so much."

"I heard that some of the MC may be there tonight. They all came roaring through town earlier today. Blade, the vice president of the club, came in to get coffees for some of the guys. He mentioned it to me."

"Blade, huh? Anything you want to tell me about this guy?"

"No. Why would you ask that?" she asks with a hint of a blush to her cheeks and annoyance in her eyes.

"No reason. Forget I asked." I reply and decide to change the subject. "Kind of surprised we never ran into them ourselves last year the few times we went out for drinks. Do they ever get rowdy?"

"They don't usually hit up any of the local bars. They have their own private bar at their clubhouse. They only mix with the town on rare occasions. I only know of a few instances where the cops were called because of a bar fight. Those were probably over a woman. Who knows?" she said as she shrugged her shoulders.

We pulled up into the parking lot and noticed how filled up it was getting. There was a long row of bikes lined up outside. "Well let's go find a table if we can. Looks really crowded already."

We walked into the bar and spotted a table near the back wall. A look around the room showed that it really was crowded in here already. So I was surprised there was an open table. As soon as we sat down, a waitress I recognized started our way. Sara Blackcat was a sweet young girl. She was just barely old enough to serve the drinks in here. Her dad, Paul, had let her start working part time after she turned 21 last year.

"Hey, you two, been a few weeks since we've seen you in here. Do the two of you always synchronize with each other with what you are going to wear?"

Bella was wearing tight blue skinny jeans with a white halter top and black boots. I was wearing black skinny jeans with a red halter top and black boots.

"Yeah took a while to get Bella to go out again. Think our last night out scared her straight for bit. And the dressing alike is always unconsciously done."

"If you could remember that night Mina, it would probably have scared you straight too! And yeah the dressing alike is what got us talking to each other the first time she ever came into the coffee shop." Bella said while laughing.

"Hahaha. I remember it just fine and it really wasn't that bad!"

"Sara please remind her that threatening bodily harm to a man twice as big as she is while swinging a wooden chair drunk off her ass, IS that bad."

"Come on! He deserved it and you both know it. Besides, Paul got there before I managed to knock his head off anyway. Paul threw him out and told him to never come back. You can't touch a female without permission and think you can get away with it." I said trying to defend my actions.

"She has a point Bella. And we all know you didn't actually want him touching you."

"You tell her Sara! Now, how has school been going? Did you finally decide on a major?"

"Not exactly…" At the same time we all heard a loud whistle from across the room and turned in that direction. Apparently some of the motorcycle club needed drinks. "Tell me what you two will have. I need to go see what Timber and the club need."

"Just bring us two beers and two shots of vodka to start. And bring us both a plate of the spaghetti and meatballs with garlic bread. Thanks Hon'." I watched her walk towards the men on the other side of the room. They were all wearing cuts that said *Wolfsbane MC*. As I watched Sara take drink orders I noticed one of the men staring straight at me. It was too far away and too dark in the bar to get a good idea of what he looked like but I could tell he was a really built man. Although I couldn't see his eyes very well, I felt like a prey animal looking into the eyes of a predator.

****

Timber

The other guys in the club talked me into going to the local bar tonight. Everyone had been mostly cooped up inside for most of the snowy season. It was finally starting to warm up so that we could enjoy some much needed time on our bikes. Although we still rode in some snowy conditions, the snow around here was too much for anything other than a four wheel drive during winter.

We had been here for about an hour with me stuck in my head thinking over a new custom build we were working on. I didn't really want to come out tonight but my club enforcer, Snake, reminded me that the President of the club needed to party with the guys on occasion and not make everything about business. Snake leaned over and said, "Come on Prez, at least pay attention and stop thinking about that fucking custom!"

"Ha-ha, you know me so well. You know I can't help it. There's only one week left until the deadline for it to be finished."

"You know we will have it finished on time. We always do." Bear said. Bear was the club accountant. Although we were a 1% club, most of our business dealings were totally legal. When I took over after my old man passed away seven years ago, I put together a plan to get us almost completely legal in all aspects of our businesses. We still sold grass and really didn't plan on stopping from doing so. It was on its way to becoming legal anyway. Once it was legal in Montana we would get a license and continue on with business as usual.

"You all damn well know, Timber won't stop thinking until we deliver it next week. By then there will be a new custom order taking up his mind." My VP, Blade, said.

"Damn it, look what just walked in boys." Snake said to everyone at the table. I looked up and felt like I was punched in the gut as all the air left my body. I was looking at the most beautiful woman I had ever seen in my life. She was wearing tight black skinny jeans and a red halter top. Even though her and the girl that walked in with her looked so much alike they could be sisters, the one in the red got my blood pumping. I kept my eyes on her the whole time they walked across the bar to a table and while they talked with Paul's daughter Sara.

"That is two very fine ass women! Don't think I have seen the one in red around before." Bear said as he and everyone else at our table stared at the two women.

I looked to my VP with a raised brow. "Blade?"

"We all know the one in white, is Bella Winters. She owns *"Bella's Brew"* in town. The one in red is her best friend, Mina Star. She moved here a year ago. There isn't much information about her other than her being a writer and that she's from a small town in Mississippi. Her record is squeaky clean."

"How the hell do you always know all this shit Blade?" asked Bear.

"Because we have a damn good enforcer that finds out about anyone new in town and reports back his findings." We all chuckled at that. Our enforcer, Snake was a wiz on a computer. He could find out just about anything he wanted to.

I continued to stare at Mina and decided I wanted to know more. We were low on beers so I whistled to get Sara's attention. Soon as she walked up I gave our orders. She went to fill them taking Mina and Bella their drinks and food first. When she returned to our table I decided to ask a few questions of my own.

"Sara, the two ladies in the back, Do you know them very well?"

"I've known Bella since I was in grade school. I met Mina when she moved here a last year. Why do you ask?" Now she was smirking at me. She knew exactly why I was asking.

Ignoring her smirk I asked "Does Mina come in here often?"

"Timber, if you want to know if the girl has a man, just straight out ask." She said while giggling at me. "The answer is no she doesn't. Neither one of them do. They hit it off with each other within days of Mina arriving in town and been best friends ever since. I haven't seen either one even go out on a date with a guy. If one of your boys asks Bella to dance though, tell them to behave themselves. Mina has a temper and will do whatever necessary to protect Bella and vice versa."

"What makes you say that?" Blade asked Sara. But Snake answered before she could.

"Last year one of the tourists was here drinking when the girls were. He grabbed Bella by the ass and Mina went nuts on him. She snatched up a chair and was about to hit him over the head. Paul came out of the back room just in time to save the fool from getting his head knocked off. Ha-ha, was the funniest shit I ever watched."

"You just watched that shit happen and didn't do anything?" Blade asks with anger in his voice. I briefly wondered what that was about.

"I took care of it." His smooth, calm answer told me all I needed to know.

"Good. Drink up boys. The night is still young." I say to all my brothers.

A round of "Hell, Yeah!" could be heard from around our tables.

Order It Here..
https://books2read.com/u/47lz7E

Night Howler's MC
Book 1
Reaper's Jewels

P*rologue*

Reaper

When a man makes a huge dumbass mistake when it comes to the woman he loves, the best thing he can do is force her back home until she forgives him. Right?

It's not like she is the only one with a reason to be pissed the fuck off. She ran off, had MY kid and was never planning to tell me about her. Yeah, I have a daughter now.

This changes things, it changes everything. I don't give a shit what I have to do, I'll pay every dime that weasel divorce lawyer is trying to get for that bitch I'm married to.

I should have done it three years ago and went after Jade when she left. But I didn't. It was the worst mistake of my life.

Hopefully Jade will forgive me for the last three years. Right now though I think she may want to kill me in my sleep. I didn't give her a choice about going   back   home.

Jade

He really thinks making me go back to North Mississippi against my will is going to help him win me back. He can go jump off the nearest cliff!

He did want me three years ago. He made that pretty damn plain. Especially when he allowed that bitch to talk to me as if I were just one of the whores that hangs around the club being passed around like a toy.

She had been gone for a couple years and everyone knew Reaper had filed for a divorce. I was so naive to think he was actually in love with me. After what happened that day and the way he acted like she was right about me being nothing to him, I know now, his feelings for me were not that deep.

I have no plans to forgive him. I know he only wants me now because we share a child. Family means everything to the Star family. And now our daughter is a part of that.

Coming Fall 2021

Chucky's Pride
A Night Howler's MC Story
Maria

Today is my first day back at work in over a month. I took an extended vacation just to get away for a while. The first week on vacation I stayed in Memphis with my best friend Rae. After all the nights spent trying to drink all the Jack Daniels in the area, I am completely surprised my liver is still working properly.

She and I spent most nights partying down on Beale Street, which is where I got my tongue pierced. I had said I was going to do it since my nineteenth birthday several months ago. At first having something like that in your mouth feels really weird, but then you get so used to it, and you forget it's even there. Well, except you find yourself twirling it around in your mouth constantly.

"Good God, I wish you'd stop doing that. It seriously looks like it would hurt," my aunt, and the boss, remarks as I walk in.

We all work in the family owned gas station. It's practically the only one in this little town. Aunt Joy is the manager, my mom is the assistant manager, and I work as a cashier. I have worked here for only about three years, but my mom and Aunt have been here longer.

"It doesn't hurt at all, Aunt Joy. You just don't like seeing it because you are a prude." I add as I stick my tongue out at her causing her to laugh.

"Kaye, can't you do something with your daughter?" she demands of my mom, who is busy stocking the shelves.

"She is twenty years old, Joy. I blame her father for the way that she is."

"You can't blame Daddy, Momma. I spent most of my childhood with you," I smile.

"Why would you get such a thing in your mouth anyway?" my mom asks.

"Because it makes *blowjobs* a little more interesting," I answer as I wag my eyebrows up and down in a suggestive way. My aunt wrinkles her nose and Mom just shakes her head and goes back to stocking the shelves. I just laugh as my Aunt Joy wrinkles her nose at me.

We hear a rumble from outside as a lone rider on a motorcycle pulls up to the gas pumps. From behind the counter, I watch as he gets off the bike and takes his helmet off. All the hair on my arms and neck stand on end as I watch him walk towards the door.

As he steps through the door, his eyes cut my way and just about suck all the air from my body. His blue eyes have me rooted to one spot.

"Bathroom?" he asks.

I vaguely hear my aunt answer his question as I am still standing there like a crazy person watching him stroll to the bathrooms.

My body has never acted like that just from looking at a man. I do have to admit that he is the most gorgeous man I have ever seen. There is just no way he's from around here. They don't grow them like that in Mississippi.

Hell, they don't grow them like that in Tennessee, either. I should know. I just spent most of my vacation there and not once found a guy that even remotely got a second look from me.

A few minutes later, he stands at the counter as I ring up the drinks and snacks he picked out.

I bite my tongue ring, swirling it outside my teeth without even paying attention. "You from around here?" I ask casually.

"I'm from all over really, but currently staying with some of my brothers on the other side of Tupelo. But, I'll be close by here for a few days. Don't know many people around here," he drawls as he looks up at me with a grin.

All I can think is, *Oh, fuck me. He has dimples.* I feel my nipples tightening up against my thin shirt, and I pray he can't see it through it.

"My name is Maria," I grin, "so now you know me. Would you like to get a drink Friday night? I know a really good bar we could go to," I add breathlessly.

"Sounds good to me," he tells me. "Everyone calls me Chucky." He holds his hand out to me palm up, and it takes me a minute to realize he wants my phone.

I watch as he calls himself and hands it back.

"I'll text ya about the details, beautiful." He grins at me as he takes his purchases and backs out the door, staring the whole way.

"Good lord, he sure was pretty. If only I were about thirty years younger," I hear from behind me.

"I thought Maria was going to pass out from the look on her face when she looked at him the first time. She didn't look like she was breathing." My mother jokes to my Aunt.

"She's still not talking, which is strange, should we check her pulse and make sure she is still alive?" asks my Aunt as I turn around to glare at them which doesn't stop them from laughing at my expense.

"Did you at least get his number?" mom finally asks.

"Better than that, I asked him out for a drink this Friday night." I finally smile wide at them both.

"Just don't do anything we wouldn't do." My aunt winks.

"Knowing you two, that doesn't leave a whole lot out." I laugh as they both huff and walk away.

I'll never get tired at riling the two of them up. For one, they make it entirely too easy to do. Even though they both love going out and having a good time, they are both still a little old fashioned about some things.

Available Now At Your Favorite Digital Store!

Other Titles by Marissa Ann

Wolfsbane Ridge MC Series

Book 1 Timber's Fairy
https://books2read.com/u/47lz7E

Book 2 Blade's Pixie
https://books2read.com/u/38RPla

Book 3 Blood's Angel
https://books2read.com/u/m2MnoG

Night Howler's MC Series, New Orleans
Book 1 Buzz
https://books2read.com/BuzzNewOrleans

Hearts of Steel Anthology featuring Wrench's
Salvation
https://books2read.com/Hearts-Of-Steel-MC-Anthology

Poison Pen Series
Book 1 Baratta's Darkness
https://books2read.com/BarattasDarkness

A Call Of Magic Limited Edition featuring
Hydra: The Dragon Keeper
https://books2read.com/callofmagic

Sea's Of Rissa, a Collection of Poems
https://books2read.com/seasofrissa

Sign Up for Marissa Ann's Newsletter
https://mailchi.mp/3ca12e9bcaec/1ex5ytjtmd

Connect with the Author

Facebook:
https://www.facebook.com/MarissaAnnAuthor
Instagram:
https://www.instagram.com/authormarissaann/
Twitter:
https://twitter.com/marissaannbooks
Goodreads:
**https://www.goodreads.com/author/show/1815985
5.Marissa_Ann**

About The Authors
Marissa Ann

Marissa Ann grew up in two very different worlds, the big city and the rural South. Mobile Alabama offered her the opportunities to not only see other cultures but to experience them as well.

Every weekend she spent most of her time on the beach of Perdido with her dog, Buddy. It didn't matter what time of the day, even midnight, they could be found walking along the shore in search of seashells.

Buddy passed away in 1997 and she still misses him today. You never forget your true best friends, even the four legged ones.

When she wasn't in Alabama with her dad, she was in North Mississippi with her mom. Mostly spending time with her Grandfather who taught her not only how to grow a garden but how to completely live off the land as well as to love animals.

Today, she spends her time in rural North Mississippi with her husband, the kids and all of their animals on a hobby farm.

She always said she would write books one day even though many thought she never would. She made a promise to a childhood friend who left this world for the next in 2015. That she would finally write and publish at least one.

Her first book hit the market in 2018 and she's never looked back. She now has several out with many more scheduled for release.

Rae Goldman

Growing up in a small Midwestern farm community, gave Rae a sheltered life. When your town has five bars, five churches and a post office there isn't much to do. So she spent her youth lost in books. She got her first babysitting job at ten years old.

By the time she graduated from high school she was working three part time jobs and had won several writing awards. One week after graduation she ran away, joining the carnival that was visiting one town over. She spent the next three years traveling the United States. Working for a traveling carnival opened her eyes to the real world. After meeting the love of her life, she settled down to raise her family in the South.

She has had many people inspire her throughout her life. The people that inspired her the most however were her teachers. She took every English and writing class her school offered. When she went back to college as an adult, she took every writing class available there also. Even though she isn't working in her degree field, writing papers every week in college prepared her for the next step.

She got to a point in her life that she felt lost; looking for direction she called her best friend. Marissa Ann said something Rae never expected. "Write a book with me." Rae had previously worked as Marissa's editor and thought she knew what she was getting into. Now her book baby is in your hands.